I0577505

PRAISE FOR DONNA GRANT'S BEST-SELLING ROMANCE NOVELS

"Grant's ability to quickly convey complicated backstory makes this jam-packed love story accessible even to new or periodic readers." - *Publisher's Weekly*

"Donna Grant has given the paranormal genre a burst of fresh air…" – *San Francisco Book Review*

"The premise is dramatic and heartbreaking; the characters are colorful and engaging; the romance is spirited and seductive." – *The Reading Cafe*

"The central romance, fueled by a hostage drama, plays out in glorious detail against a backdrop of multiple ongoing issues in the "Dark Kings" books. This seemingly penultimate installment creates a nice segue to a climactic end." – *Library Journal*

"…intense romance amid the growing war between the Dragons and the Dark Fae is scorching hot." – *Booklist*

DON'T MISS THESE OTHER NOVELS BY

NYT & USA Today bestselling author DONNA GRANT

<u>CONTEMPORARY PARANORMAL</u>

DRAGON KINGS® SERIES

Dragon Revealed ~ Dragon Mine ~ Dragon Unbound
Dragon Eternal ~ Dragon Lover ~ Dragon Arisen
Ignite the Magic (Prequel)

SKYE DRUIDS SERIES

Iron Ember ~ Shoulder the Skye ~ Heart of Glass

DARK UNIVERSE HEAs

Bundled Collections
A Dragon's Tale: Whisky and Wishes, Heart of Gold, &
Of Fire and Flame ~ Holiday Heat: Dark Alpha's Silent Night,
My Fiery Valentine, Shards of Hope, A Warrior for Christmas

REAPER SERIES

Dark Alpha's Claim ~ Dark Alpha's Embrace
Dark Alpha's Demand ~ Books 1-3: Tall Dark Deadly Alpha
Dark Alpha's Lover ~ Dark Alpha's Night
Dark Alpha's Hunger ~ Dark Alpha's Awakening
Dark Alpha's Redemption ~ Dark Alpha's Temptation
Dark Alpha's Caress ~ Dark Alpha's Obsession
Dark Alpha's Need ~ Dark Alpha's Silent Night
Dark Alpha's Passion ~ Dark Alpha's Command
Dark Alpha's Fury

DARK KINGS SERIES

Dark Heat ~ Darkest Flame ~ Fire Rising ~ Burning Desire
Hot Blooded ~ Night's Blaze ~ Soul Scorched ~ Dragon King
Passion Ignites ~ Smoldering Hunger ~ Smoke and Fire
Dragon Fever ~ Firestorm ~ Blaze ~ Dragon Burn ~ Torched
Dragon Night ~ Dragonfire ~ Dragon Claimed ~ Ignite
Constantine: A History Bundle ~ Fever ~ Dragon Lost
Flame ~ Inferno ~ My Fiery Valentine ~ The Dragon King
Coloring Book ~ Dragon King Special Edition Character
Coloring Book: Rhi ~ Ignite the Magic (Prequel)

DARK WARRIORS SERIES

Midnight's Master ~ Midnight's Lover ~ Midnight's Seduction
Midnight's Warrior ~ Midnight's Kiss ~ Midnight's Captive
Midnight's Temptation ~ Midnight's Promise
Midnight's Surrender ~ A Warrior for Christmas

CHIASSON SERIES

Wild Fever ~ Wild Dream ~ Wild Need
Wild Flame ~ Wild Rapture ~ Chiasson Series Bundle

LARUE SERIES

Moon Kissed ~ Moon Thrall ~ Moon Struck ~ Moon Bound
LaRue Series Bundle

DARK BEGINNINGS: A FIRST IN SERIES BOXSET

Chiasson Series, Book 1: Wild Fever
LaRue Series, Book 1: Moon Kissed
The Royal Chronicles Series, Book 1: Prince of Desire

HISTORICAL PARANORMAL

THE KINDRED SERIES

Everkin ~ Eversong ~ Everwylde ~ Everbound
Evernight ~ Everspell

KINDRED: THE FATED SERIES

Rage ~ Ruin ~ Reign

DARK SWORD SERIES

Dangerous Highlander ~ Forbidden Highlander
Wicked Highlander ~ Untamed Highlander
Shadow Highlander ~ Darkest Highlander

ROGUES OF SCOTLAND SERIES

The Craving ~ The Hunger ~ The Tempted ~ The Seduced
Rogues of Scotland Box Set

THE SHIELDS SERIES

A Dark Guardian ~ A Kind of Magic ~ A Dark Seduction
A Forbidden Temptation ~ A Warrior's Heart
Mystic Trinity (a series connecting novel)

DRUIDS GLEN SERIES

Highland Mist ~ Highland Nights ~ Highland Dawn
Highland Fires ~ Highland Magic
Mystic Trinity (a series connecting novel)

SISTERS OF MAGIC TRILOGY

Shadow Magic ~ Echoes of Magic ~ Dangerous Magic

Sisters of Magic Box Set

THE ROYAL CHRONICLES SERIES

Prince of Desire ~ Prince of Seduction

Prince of Love ~ Prince of Passion

The Royal Chronicles Box Set

Mystic Trinity (a series connecting novel)

WICKED TREASURES

Seized by Passion ~ Enticed by Ecstasy ~ Captured by Desire

Wicked Treasures Box Set

MILITARY ROMANCE / ROMANTIC SUSPENSE

SONS OF TEXAS SERIES

The Hero ~ The Protector ~ The Legend

The Defender ~ The Guardian

<u>**COWBOY / CONTEMPORARY**</u>

<u>**HEART OF TEXAS SERIES**</u>
The Christmas Cowboy Hero ~ Cowboy, Cross My Heart
My Favorite Cowboy ~ A Cowboy Like You
Looking for a Cowboy ~ A Cowboy Kind of Love

<u>**STAND ALONE BOOKS**</u>
That Cowboy of Mine
Home for a Cowboy Christmas
Forever Mine
Savage Moon

**Check out Donna Grant's Online Store at
www.DonnaGrant.com/shop
for autographed books, character
themed goodies, and more!**

This is a work of fiction. All of the characters, organizations, and events portrayed in this novel are either products of the author's imagination or are used fictitiously.

HOLIDAY HEAT
© 2023 by DL Grant, LLC
Cover Design © 2023 by Charity Hendry Designs
Formatting © 2023 by Charity Hendry Designs
ISBN 13: 978-1-958353-20-2
Available in ebook, print, and audio.
All rights reserved.

Glimpse from: **IGNITE THE MAGIC**
© 2023 by DL Grant, LLC
Cover Design © 2023 by Charity Hendry Designs

Peek from: **HEART OF GLASS**
© 2023 by DL Grant, LLC
Cover Design © 2023 by Charity Hendry Designs

All rights reserved, including the right to reproduce or transmit this book, or a portion thereof, in any form or by any means, electronic or mechanical, without permission in writing from the author. This book may not be resold or uploaded for distribution to others. Thank you for respecting the hard work of this author.

www.DonnaGrant.com
www.MotherofDragonsBooks.com

A DARK UNIVERSE HEA SET

HOLIDAY HEAT

NYT & USA TODAY BESTSELLING AUTHOR

DONNA GRANT

A REAPER NOVELLA
part of the DARK WORLD

DARK ALPHA'S SILENT NIGHT

NEW YORK TIMES BESTSELLING AUTHOR

DONNA GRANT

CHAPTER ONE

Death's Realm

River sighed as she softly closed the door to her son's room after finally getting him to nap. Once Breac had learned to walk, he was everywhere. She spent most of her time chasing him from one place to another. Since he was three-quarters Fae, she knew he had magic. He hadn't used any—yet. But it was coming. She might be a Halfling, but even though she was part Fae, she had been raised in the human world without any magic.

"You look exhausted."

She turned at the sound of her husband's sexy Irish accent, which was so different than her Scottish one. Her gaze met his black-ringed red eyes. He had his shoulder-length, silver-laced black hair pulled into a queue at the base of his neck. He was, by far, the most handsome man she had ever seen.

"The first time I saw you, I was struck by just how enigmatically gorgeous you were," she told him.

He raised black brows, a slow smile pulling at his lips. "Is that so?"

She nodded and walked to him, letting her fingers caress his hollowed cheek down to the hard line of his jaw. "Oh, yes. I tried to come off like my heart didn't miss a beat when I saw you, but I don't think I managed it."

Kyran wrapped his arms around her. "I couldn't say since I was too busy looking through the horrible frumpy disguise to your beauty beneath. As if baggy clothes and glasses could hide your stunning face."

She sighed as he pulled her tightly against him and rested her cheek on his chest as her arms wound around him. River hadn't truly come alive or begun living until she met Kyran. She hadn't wanted any part of the Reapers or their problems. But it was as if her destiny had been intertwined with Kyran's eons ago. And she was thankful for it.

Sure, there had been danger and enemies and more close calls than she was comfortable with, but the one thing she knew above all else was that Kyran loved her and their son.

"What are you thinking about?" he asked as he leaned back and looked at her, concern sparking in his crimson eyes.

River tucked strands of her hair behind her ear. "Nothing."

He quirked a brow and simply stared at her, waiting. They had a steadfast rule in their relationship: they didn't keep anything from each other. Ever.

She licked her lips and glanced away. "My pregnancy was a surprise for both of us."

"Aye," he replied gently, his gaze never leaving her face.

"I just…" Her stomach felt tied in knots as she bit her lip and pulled out of his arms. River didn't get far. Kyran tenderly stopped her.

"Babe? What is it? You know you can tell me anything."

His worry was deepening. This was why she hadn't brought anything up before now. "Breac is the only child here. Not having other children to be around and play with can harm him. Not only that, but he's more Fae than human. I'm not sure what to expect as far as what his magic will be or how he'll use it. We're safe here. I can't thank Erith enough for opening her realm to not only her Reapers but also the rest of us."

"Rest of you?" Kyran flattened his lips. "You're my mate. My wife. Of course, you and the other mates are welcome."

She covered her face with her hands as she struggled to put into words the emotions that had begun to grow inside her for weeks. After a deep breath, she let her arms fall to her sides and looked at him. "I need to preface this by saying a lot of what I'm feeling has to do with the Fae Others who are trying to kill you and the other Reapers." She paused to swallow. "I miss things I took for granted on Earth. I miss celebrating the holidays. I miss setting up a Christmas tree and decorating it. I long to go shopping to find gifts for everyone. I want to see Breac sitting on the floor, tearing open his presents as he hurries to find what's beneath the paper."

"Is that all?" Kyran said with a relieved sigh.

She blinked, taken aback by his flippant reply. "Is that *all*?"

He visibly winced. "I didn't mean that your feelings aren't

important, sweetheart. I braced myself for you telling me you wanted to leave."

"Never," she said and rose on tiptoe to place her lips on his. "My home is wherever you are."

He rubbed his hands up and down her arms. "How do you want to solve this problem? I can have everything you want with a snap of my fingers."

"I know."

"Then why haven't you asked, love?" he asked, frowning.

River sighed. Why *hadn't* she asked? There were a million different reasons. The Reapers had a little respite, but it wouldn't last long. She didn't want to take away the slice of time they had to pour her troubles out when they should be enjoying each other. "I've just been overwhelmed by a lot of emotions lately."

"You shouldn't have kept them to yourself. We promised to talk about everything."

"You're right. I thought maybe I was just overthinking things. But the more I kept it to myself, the more it festered."

He lightly brushed his knuckles against her cheek. "No more of that. We can start on the holiday stuff anytime you want. I was on Earth a long time before I became a Reaper. I should've realized you and the other Halflings might be missing home."

"We're grateful to be safe. A lot's been going on. I didn't want to add something frivolous to the real issues."

"Anything that causes you anxiety isn't frivolous."

She smiled, her heart full of his love. "Thank you."

"Do you want to talk to the other mates? Or should we do the holidays ourselves?"

"Let me talk to them. Ever since we went to Dreagan for their holiday dinner last year, I've wanted to do something similar."

Kyran laughed, his eyes crinkling. "Have at it, love. I'll support you however you need."

"If you'll watch Breac, I'll talk to the girls now."

He didn't release her, and his smile died. "There were other things you spoke about. Grave concerns you had regarding our son."

"He's still young. Maybe we don't need to worry about them now."

"River."

She briefly squeezed her eyes closed. "I don't know the answer, babe."

"Do you want another child?"

"No. Maybe. I don't know," she said in irritation. "That wasn't what I meant."

"I understand your apprehension about Breac being an only child and the only child on the realm. As for the magic part, that is something I can help you with."

He looked as if he wanted to say more, but he held back. River shook her head. "Nope. If you made me talk, then you must, as well. Spill it."

There was a hint of a smile before Kyran said, "I'd never thought about children, not once I became a Reaper. We were never supposed to love. After Erith changed her rules, I was too overjoyed to have found you to even think too much about what our future might hold."

"Then we discovered I was pregnant."

He nodded solemnly. "All while battling enemies."

"We're still contending with them."

"We're safe here. No one knows about this place."

She glanced down at her hands that rested on his chest. "You might be stronger, faster, and more powerful than normal Fae, but you can still be killed. Every time you leave, I know the Others might find you and attack."

"There will always be adversaries and danger. Erith chose me as one of her Reapers because of my skills. I don't want to spend our lives worrying about what-ifs instead of being happy."

River had to admit that he had a point. "What is it you want?"

"Another child with you. A little sister, perhaps, for Breac," Kyran said with a smile.

She found her lips curving to match his. "As if I could ever refuse anything you want."

"We'll finish this conversation later. I'll watch our son while you talk to the girls. Then, when you get back, we're decorating the house. We should've done it weeks ago."

He gave her a long, slow kiss before slapping her on the ass as she walked away. River glanced over her shoulder and winked at him as she left their house. She still couldn't believe she had fallen in love with a Reaper. Being a Halfling—half-human, half-Fae—had made for a difficult life growing up. She didn't belong in the Fae world because her blood was tainted. The human world only saw the beauty of a Fae and tried to exploit it. That's why she had attempted to hide who she was. Not to mention, she had gotten the family's gift. The ability to read ancient Fae languages. Something that only happened once a generation.

She learned not just of her family's legacy but also how to defend herself. She'd had no choice but to become a warrior. River both hated and liked that she had Fae blood. Since Kyran, she had come to terms with who she was and how she could use it to help Death and the Reapers.

Her steps were light as she walked. Death's realm was picturesque in every sense of the word. Every single place on the realm was jaw-droppingly gorgeous. She and Kyran had settled on a section of rolling hills near a loch. The minute he saw it, he just stopped and stared. He hadn't had to say a word. It was clear he was taken by it. She had known immediately that this was where he wanted to have a home.

After he became a Reaper, he and the others had moved about constantly, setting up temporary quarters on Earth. He hadn't had a real home in many centuries. Seeing how enamored he was with the location made it the perfect place for their home. The other Reapers found similar places.

Some were farther from the white tower that Erith and Cael used as their home, but she and Kyran were one of the closest to it. She didn't have the ability to teleport as the Reapers did, so she had to walk. River enjoyed having the time to herself—and the exercise. She shivered slightly in the cool, damp air, deciding that before she did anything, she should speak to Erith. This was Death's realm, after all.

Forty minutes later, River reached the white tower. She lifted her hand to knock, but the door opened before she got the chance. She found herself staring into Cael's purple eyes. The once-Light Fae had previously been the leader of Kyran's group of Reapers. After an altercation with one of his enemies where he nearly died—only to be saved by Erith's magic—he'd been transformed into a god.

"River," Cael greeted her with a smile. "What brings you to our door?"

"I was hoping I could talk with you and Erith."

He stepped aside so she could enter. "Of course."

River glanced up at the curving staircase that ran along one of the tower's walls, all the way to the very top. She spotted Erith midway up, making her way down the steps. Her long, blue-black hair was in a loose plait over one shoulder. The petite goddess effortlessly glided down the steps in an all-black outfit that was a cross between *Xena: Warrior Princess* and Hela from *Thor*. Somehow, Erith pulled it off in only a manner that Death could.

"What can we do for you?" Erith asked when she reached the bottom.

River took a deep breath and said, "I'm missing some of the things we did on Earth. I was hoping to throw a holiday dinner like what Con and Rhi did at Dreagan. Just for us here," she hastily added.

Erith's lavender gaze briefly moved to Cael before she said, "I think that would be delightful. With everything we've been dealing with, I'm sorry to say I haven't thought about what those of you who came here left behind."

"You have our gratitude for opening your home to us. We might miss a few things from Earth, but that can be remedied."

Cael walked to stand beside Erith. "I think a dinner party is just what we need."

"Yes," Erith said with a smile that didn't quite reach her eyes.

River understood. Their enemies had gotten powerful. Then there was the fact they chasing Xaneth—a royal Fae who had helped them. On top of that, Aisling had gone in search of him. Erith wasn't just looking for one person now but two. All of that weighed heavily on her slim shoulders.

That's when River realized that it wasn't just her that needed a night to remember what they had. Erith did, too.

All of them did.

CHAPTER TWO

River tugged the sleeves of her sweater over her hands as the brush of a cool breeze rushed by her. It was winter on the realm, but Erith had set her tower and the Fae doorway in a temperate area. It made for mild seasons. Though River had to admit, she missed the snowfall during the winter.

As she made her way to Neve and Talin's cottage, her mind swirled with possibilities for the party. She couldn't believe that she had held off talking about it. But that's what happened when she let her mind come up with reasons for keeping it to herself. Her steps quickened in her excitement.

Neve answered the door with a smile, her long, straight black hair pulled into a low ponytail. Her silver eyes that identified her as a Light Fae brightened at the sight of River. "Hey! I was just thinking about you."

"Really?" River asked as she walked inside.

"I was thinking we need a girls' day."

"That does sound good."

Neve motioned for her to follow as she led River from the entryway into the living area. "Would you like something to drink?"

"I'm fine, thanks. I'm actually here to talk to you about something."

"Oh, I'm all ears. Sit."

River sank into the contemporary white leather chair next to the light gray sofa while Neve tucked a foot under her and curled up on the couch in a corner. River glanced at the fire that popped, warming the room. "I want to host a holiday dinner party this year. It's last-minute, but I've been missing things I would normally do this time of year."

"That sounds fun. Is there anything I can help with?"

River smiled and scooted to the edge of the chair. "I was hoping you'd ask."

They shared a laugh before Neve asked, "What are the details?"

"I don't know," River admitted with a shake of her head. "I just came from talking to Erith and Cael to make sure they were okay with it."

Neve rolled her eyes. "Of course, they are, but it was good that you spoke to them. So…dates?"

"Christmas Eve."

"You mean, in two days? Have you told everyone?"

"Not yet. I was hoping you could help me with that since you can get around faster than I can."

Neve laughed. "It would be my pleasure. Are you hosting it?"

"I wanted to, but I'd like it to feel like the holidays. Snow and all that. It doesn't snow at my place."

Neve's eyes widened. "I have the perfect location. Talin and I found it months ago."

"Where?" River asked.

Neve jumped to her feet and held out her hand. "It's better if I show you."

Later that evening, Kyran studied River from his position on the edge of the sofa.

"What?" she asked with a grin from her place on the floor next to Breac, who stood between them.

"You're really not going to tell me the location?"

She shook her head, her eyes glinting with merriment. "It's a surprise."

"Who all knows the place?"

"Stop," she said with a laugh. "You can wait a few days to find out."

He flattened his lips and sighed. "You know I have no patience."

"Exactly. This will be good for you."

Kyran snorted. "I doubt you'd be amenable if the situation were reversed."

"I know I wouldn't," she replied pithily.

His attention shifted to their son, who had his eye on something across the room. Just as Breac took off, Kyran snatched him, lifting the child high as he got to his feet before spinning him around. Breac squealed in delight, his little laugh bouncing off the walls. Kyran kissed Breac on the cheek before setting him back on the floor to continue playing as he resumed his seat.

"I'm not leaving you out."

He lifted his gaze to River's pale blue eyes. "I know."

"I want this to be special for you."

"Babe, everything we do together is special."

She narrowed her eyes at him. "Nice try. I'm still not telling you."

"It was worth a try," he said with a grin.

Breac reached for a strand of River's long, straight dark hair. She flicked it over her shoulder and tickled Breac to shift his focus. Kyran realized that his mate had a knack for knowing how to do that for both him and their son. Not that he minded. Her excitement warmed his heart.

He'd been more than a little worried after their conversation that morning. It had been obvious that something was on her mind, but he had assumed it was the growing tension regarding the Fae Others. He'd never realized that she missed her home—though he should have.

Kyran smiled at his son and briefly met his wife's eyes. Being on Death's realm might keep the mates and his son safe, but he and the other Reapers needed to remember that some had given up their homes to be with them.

"Do you regret it?" he asked.

River's head swung to him. "What?"

"Us. Leaving your home."

She rose to her feet and walked to him, pushing him back so she could sit on his lap. Her pale blue eyes held his as she touched his face with her hand. "I regret nothing. If I had the chance to do it all again, I wouldn't change a thing. I love you with all my heart. I might miss things about

Earth, but the comfort and safety of living here is well worth it."

"You'll tell me if that changes?"

"I promise," she whispered before lowering her head and placing her lips on his.

Kyran's blood heated as his arms tightened around her. He hadn't thought it possible to love someone as he loved his wife, but there was no denying that they had a special bond that couldn't be explained.

"Me!" Breac cried.

Kyran and River broke apart to look down at their son, who stood beside the sofa, staring up at them with a bright smile. River reached down and lifted him, placing him on her lap. Breac laughed as he looked from her to Kyran. The simplest things brought his son joy—and gave Kyran more things to smile about.

"I've got to go," River said, though she made no move to leave.

Kyran grinned. "It's misting."

She laughed and ran her fingers through his hair. "That won't stop me."

"Let me and Breac bring you."

"How can I resist that offer from my handsome men?"

Kyran looked at Breac. "Did you hear that, son? She thinks we're handsome."

Breac smiled in response.

Kyran took his son while River rose from his lap and put on her boots. When she was ready, he got to his feet and tucked Breac against him before holding his hand out to River. As soon as she took it, he teleported the three of them under the overhang at the entrance of Talin's house. The door opened before either could knock.

"Breac!" Neve said in a high-pitched voice when she saw the boy.

Breac's face lit up as he reached for his Aunt Neve. Kyran handed over his son, watching as his plump little arms wrapped around Neve's neck and squeezed, his fingers tangling in her hair. Neve smothered Breac in kisses and motioned Kyran and River in. Neve didn't get too far before Talin came around the corner, likely drawn by the sound of Breac's laughter.

"There's my little man," Talin said.

Breac pressed his open mouth against Neve's cheek, then held out his arms to Talin. Kyran watched as his fellow Reaper plucked Breac from his mate's arms and swung him up high, causing Breac to squeal in delight. He was used to being passed from person to person when the others were around, and Breac liked the attention.

"Not fair," Neve said to her husband. "I just got Breac. You're going to have him for a while."

Talin grinned, his silver eyes mischievous. "Then let us stay."

"Nope," River said before Neve could.

Neve sighed. "She's right. You two have to go. But you can leave Breac."

"I think it's better if he comes with us," Kyran said as he caught Talin's gaze. His friend gave a barely discernable nod.

"We'll leave you girls to it," Talin said as he walked to his mate and gave her a soft kiss. "Don't do anything I wouldn't do."

Neve rolled her eyes. "You would do anything and everything."

"Exactly," Talin said with a flash of a smile.

Kyran kissed River before he and Talin returned to his home. He rubbed his hands together. "It's time to get started."

"Started?" Talin said as he set Breac down once the boy spotted his toys again.

"The girls might have a plan, but so do I."

Talin straightened. "Now I'm intrigued."

Kyran held up a hand as he called the others. One by one, the Reapers arrived. The only one missing was Aisling. As much as Kyran hoped she would come, he knew that as long as she searched for Xaneth, she wouldn't. No one knew why Erith allowed Aisling to track Xaneth, but none of them questioned Death.

Kyran looked around at the room, his gaze moving from Baylon, Fintan, Daire, Eoghan, Cael, Bradach, Dubhan, Cathal, Rordan, Torin, and Balladyn. "Most of you already know that River is planning a holiday dinner party. The girls want it to be a surprise for us. That gave me the idea to surprise them, as well."

Dubhan crossed his arms over his chest. His long, black and silver hair pulled into a queue. "I'm game. What are you thinking?"

"River misses Earth and all that goes along with this season. I have a feeling she isn't the only one," Kyran said.

Fintan ran a hand through his long, white hair. "Aye. Cat misses it, too."

"Sorcha also," Cathal said with a nod of his black and silver head.

Kyran looked at Daire, Baylon, and Eoghan, all of whom nodded that their mates felt the same as his. "Even those who aren't Halflings lived on Earth long enough to know the holiday season. We've been so wrapped up in our duties and fighting enemies that we've forgotten about those who gave up everything to be with us."

"Do you have a plan?" Cael asked, a smile on his lips.

Kyran wrinkled his nose. "Not exactly."

Baylon and Daire started laughing, elbowing each other.

Fintan gave them a withering stare before looking at Kyran. "We need to think about what humans do during this season."

"What we need is to know what the girls are doing so we don't do the same thing," Kyran said.

Everyone looked at Cael.

He rolled his eyes at them and then bent to lift Breac, who was tugging on his pant leg. "I'll see what I can find out. Don't expect much."

Kyran rubbed his hands together again. "We need to make a list. We don't have that long, and we're going to have to work while the girls are together. I don't want them to know anything."

For the next hour, they passed Breac around, taking turns feeding and playing with him as they thought up ideas that Kyran put into a list. This would be the best holiday River ever had.

CHAPTER THREE

The walls reverberated with conversations and laughter. Erith gazed around the room at the women who had become her family. For eons, she had watched others, longing for friendship and sisterhood.

And now, she finally had it.

She had been surprised and delighted when the invite had come, asking her to join the planning session for the holiday party. Though, she had to admit, she wasn't sure she fit in. She kept telling herself to relax. Erith finally understood the term *fish out of water*.

River let out a whistle to gain everyone's attention. The room quieted instantly as everyone turned to her with expressions of interest and excitement. Erith found her lips curving into a smile, her anticipation palpable.

"I'm so happy to see all of you here," River said. "There's a lot to do, and not a lot of time to do it."

Fianna chuckled. "Good thing there's a few Fae and a goddess among us. We'll get it all done. Don't worry."

There was a round of laughter as heads nodded and many glanced in Erith's direction.

River licked her lips and scooted to the edge of the sofa cushion, a pad of paper in her hands. "I know we all enjoyed the party at Dreagan last year. I don't know if the Dragon Kings will have another one, but I thought it would be good if we did something for our family."

"Stop," Jordyn said in her Scots brogue as she wiped at the corner of her turquoise eye. "You're going to make me cry."

Ettie, who sat beside Jordyn, nudged her with a shoulder and said in an Irish accent, "Trust me. We'll all be crying at some point."

"This is a great idea, River. Thank you," Maeve replied. The Light Fae bowed her head of black hair with its silver accents in gratitude.

Catriona sniffed loudly and glared at Maeve with her green gaze. "Bloody hell. Should we just cry now and get it over with?"

Erith laughed with the others. It warmed her heart to see so many Halflings and Fae together. Her family. She had kept the Reapers from falling in love for so long, but then she realized that some things couldn't be denied. She was delighted that she had set aside that rule because look what she had now. She would do anything for her Reapers.

And she would do anything for the mates and little Breac, too.

Anything.

They were her family.

"Okay," River said to get everyone back on track. "We need to come up with an aesthetic."

Sorcha shoved aside her auburn curls and shrugged before saying in an Irish accent, "It's your party. You get to choose."

"I agree," Thea, another Irish Halfling, replied.

One by one, they nodded in agreement.

Erith was surprised to find River's eyes on her. She grinned at the Scottish Halfling. "Your party, your colors."

"But this isn't about me," River argued. "It's about all of us."

"This year, you pick the colors. For the following years, we'll vote," Erith offered.

Light Fae, Kyra, quickly said, "I *love* that idea."

"Perfect," Neve replied and turned her head to River, who sat beside her. "It's decided. You pick."

River twisted her lips. "Um…okay," she said hesitantly. "We could use traditional red and green. Or there's red and white, blue and silver, red and silver, silver and gold, burgundy and gold, green and–"

"Which one do you like the best?" Breda asked, her Irish accent thick.

River sighed, and then a slow smile spread over her face. "White and gold with red accents."

There were *oohs* and *aahs* at her choice.

With that decision made, it seemed to propel River. "I'd like this to feel as festive as it can. Neve showed me an amazing spot today on one of the mountains. There will be lots of snow to complement everything."

"Please tell me this isn't going to be outside," Ettie said with a wrinkle of her nose.

Neve shook her head. "Absolutely not. I've got some ideas for the building, but I've been waiting to hear everything River had planned."

"Thank goodness for magic," Jordyn said with a laugh.

River nodded and checked something off on her notepad. "We're going to need a table large enough to hold all of us, along with chairs. Yes, I'm counting Aisling because I really hope she makes it back for this."

Sadness tinged the atmosphere for Erith at the thought of Aisling being gone, but also for Balladyn. The two of them were the only ones who weren't mated.

"I'd like to do the table and chairs," Maeve offered.

River smiled and checked off something else. "Perfect. Thanks. Next, I'm going to need side tables for all the food. I'm thinking one for desserts, one for drinks, one for hors d'oeuvres, three for food."

Breda raised her hand. "I've got that."

Another checkmark. River looked up. "Lights. Inside and out."

"Oh, me," Fianna said excitedly.

River laughed with the others and made another mark on the paper. "That brings me to the paths. Obviously, we'll be teleporting there, but I'd still like some outside places where we can perhaps have a firepit and a cozy seating area."

"That's right up my alley," Kyra replied. "I'd like to do that."

River looked directly at Erith again. "I was hoping you might do the flowers."

To say that Erith was delighted, was an understatement. "Of course."

"Wonderful," River said with a bright smile. "We'll be using our Fae sisters for the rest, but…" She drew out the word as she looked at the other five Halflings. "There's a huge list here of things that need to be done."

Sorcha said, "I'd love to put together the menu."

"Oh! Can I do the desserts?" Cat asked.

"Check and check," River said as she marked the pad.

Erith's heart warmed as everyone joined in to put their touches on every part of the dinner. With each minute that passed, her excitement for the party grew because she knew it would be a spectacular event.

"Well?" River asked the others after they had teleported to the top of the mountain.

Everyone was huddled in thick jackets with scarves, mittens, and beanies. She imagined she had worn a similar expression of amazement and shock when Neve had brought her here earlier. She exchanged a look with Neve, a smile on each of their lips. The location was breathtaking.

"Told you," she whispered.

River nodded. "This will definitely feel like the holidays."

"Right here," Kyra said as she walked to a spot about thirty feet from the edge of the cliff and held her arms about a few inches from her hips, turning in a slow circle. "This is where the firepit needs to be. Have seating surrounding it so this view can be enjoyed from every angle."

A shiver ran through River that had nothing to do with the cold and everything to do with the anticipation. "Yes."

Neve had taken several steps back, her gaze trained on the area adjacent to Kyra's. "There's plenty of room for whatever size building we want. I'd like it to blend in with the surroundings. A cabin look of wood and stone. Lots of big windows to enjoy the spectacular views, and a vaulted ceiling."

There were words of agreement.

Neve looked at River, who nodded. In a blink, the building was there, just as Neve described. Everyone hurried inside. River gasped at the rustic beauty that surrounded them. The walls were wood, painted white with bronze patina that matched the stain on the wood floors and the ceiling beams and trim. The ceiling was high above them with one large, oval chandelier in the center of the room, bearing dozens of small lights. Smaller, matching sconces adorned the walls.

River could've looked at it forever. But Neve's creation spurred the others. In moments, Kyra had used her magic to construct a large outdoor area using flagstones as the base. The design followed the natural edge of the mountain. A massive bowl-shaped copper firepit sat in the middle with bronze and gold glass rocks. Around the pit, she'd placed two semi-circular sofas that gave off a Nordic vibe, each piled with pillows and fur blankets.

Just as River took all of that in, she heard more gasps. She rushed back into the building and saw the dining room. Her mouth dropped at the dark stain of the rustic yet elegant table with the live edge. It was as unique as it was beautiful. The tall-backed cream chairs were tufted, giving the room a formal look.

"Kyra, the outside is breathtaking. Maeve, the table and

chairs are stunning," River said, her eyes watering with emotion.

Breda flashed a smile and waggled her brows. "My turn."

With a snap of her fingers, the side tables River had requested appeared along the walls. They were the same shade as the dining table and had white runners with festive designs along the edges in gold thread.

River clapped in her excitement. "Yes, yes!"

Then, everyone looked at Fianna for the lights. She shook her head. "Not yet. I've got a surprise for all of you."

"Same," Erith said with a wink.

River tried to hide her disappointment, but she also realized that everyone was excited about the dinner and wanted to put their own spin on it. The dinner was tomorrow night. That was enough time to put the finishing touches on everything.

"We haven't talked about what to wear," Neve said.

Jordyn laughed. "Cocktail attire, of course."

"Don't forget, we need to buy the guys presents," Ettie stated.

Maeve shrugged, grinning. "That's what we're for."

"What about a tree?" Sorcha asked. "Are we going to have a decorated tree?"

River clutched her pad of paper against her chest as everyone turned to her. "Absolutely. Right there," she said and pointed to the corner to her left between two windows.

Without hesitation, Erith asked, "Flocked? Green? Or another color?"

"Green," River replied.

In the next heartbeat, a twenty-foot fir tree stood in the

corner. Boxes of white, gold, and red ornaments of various sizes and shapes appeared all over the place. Lengths of lighted garland waited to be hung.

River pointed to the wall where it met the ceiling. "Drape the garland all the way around."

Before the words had left her mouth, it was up and lit.

"How about these?" Kyra asked as she held up clear glass beads that would reflect the lights.

River nodded.

Once the beads were on the garland, clusters of white and gold ornaments were added, nearly weighing the garland down. Four matching wreaths hung on the inside of the two sets of double doors. And then everyone turned to the tree.

River didn't know which of the Fae was producing the ornaments, and it didn't matter. They were having fun putting everything on the tree. They had suffered so much in such a short time. And while they had bonded through danger, they were now connecting in a different way.

All too soon, the tree was finished. River was shocked to find Neve handing her a gold tree skirt trimmed in white fur. She carefully wrapped the tree's base and then stepped back to look at the lit beauty. Only then did she realize that something was missing.

"We need a topper," she said.

Breda moved forward. "How about this?"

A large, gold Moravian star suddenly sat atop the tree. River beamed at Breda. "It's perfect."

"Time for presents," Fianna called.

Each Halfling went to a Fae or Erith to choose their present for their mate. In no time, there were gifts of all sizes wrapped in gold, white, and red paper with coordinating bows beneath the tree.

"We're not done, ladies," Kyra said. "Dress time."

The building erupted in laughter as they gathered together once more.

CHAPTER FOUR

Early that next morning, Kyran left to meet up with the rest of the Reapers in a wooded area on a mountain coated with freshly fallen snow. Not even Cael knew the location where River was planning the dinner, but he had an approximate area. That was enough.

"This was a great idea," Daire told Kyran. "The girls are going to be so surprised."

It had taken some doing, but Cael had come through for them. Erith hadn't told him exactly what was happening, but she had given him enough that Kyran's plan could be implemented.

"I have to agree," Cael said.

Kyran looked around at his fellow Reapers, a smile on his face—until his gaze landed on Balladyn. He and Aisling were the only unmated Reapers. When Kyran had put together his plan, he had forgotten about them. Since Aisling wasn't there, he hadn't factored her into things. But he should have thought of Balladyn.

The former King of the Dark stood with the others but slightly behind them as if he weren't really a part of the group. Kyran had his own complicated past with Balladyn. Kyran's family had betrayed him, but Balladyn had taken his life. For a long time, Kyran had hated the Dark for his role in his death. As centuries passed, Kyran's anger faded. Especially as people betrayed Balladyn time and again.

If Kyran hadn't been deceived and killed, he wouldn't have become a Reaper. He would never have found the love of his life. Whatever resentment used to reside within him was gone. He had suffered—every Reaper had.

But few as horribly as Balladyn.

"What's the plan?" Dubhan asked.

Kyran cleared his throat when Balladyn's red eyes met his. Kyran looked away and forced a smile. "We're going to take the girls on a walk. We need to find an area that's perfect so we can clear it. From there, we'll each find a tree and get it set up along the path. Baylon, you'll be first."

"Because I found love first," he said with a smirk.

Eoghan let out a snort. "We'll let you believe that."

Kyran chuckled with the rest. "Once you have your spot and your tree decorated, you need to come up with a gift for your mate. There'll be a second gift. A custom ornament to add to the largest tree at the end of the walk."

Cathal rubbed his hands together. "Can we get started?"

"Go," Kyran said.

Some Reapers teleported away, and others walked in

different directions. Just as Balladyn turned, Kyran called out his name.

He walked to the Dark Fae. "I need to apologize."

"For what?" Balladyn asked.

"You know what. I was focused on doing something for River, and that naturally translated to the others who are mated."

"And I'm not."

Kyran nodded. "I didn't mean to leave you out."

"You think because I don't have someone that I feel excluded?"

"Aye."

Balladyn's lips softly curled into a grin. "Don't worry about me. I'm just fine."

Kyran stared after him. Regardless of Balladyn's words, he was worried. In his effort to do something special, had he pushed Balladyn out even more? It wasn't his intention, but Kyran suspected that he would be trying to make it up to Balladyn for a long time.

"I'll look out for him," Cael said as he walked up.

Kyran turned to his leader and met his purple eyes. "I fekked up."

"Your heart was in the right place. Balladyn knows that. It's why he isn't upset."

"I would be. We're all couples here."

Cael lifted one shoulder in a half-shrug. "It wouldn't be so bad if Aisling were here. Focus on your tree for River. Let me worry about the rest."

Kyran reluctantly agreed. He glanced over to find that

Fintan had Breac. The Dark warrior nodded, letting Kyran know that he would keep his son safe. Even as he walked through the snow, his attention became divided between the happiness he and so many of the Reapers had found, and the two who hadn't. Everyone was worried about Xaneth. The royal Light Fae had helped them when they battled a formidable enemy, but then he had disappeared. They'd discovered too late that it was Usaeil, Xaneth's aunt and the Queen of the Light, who had captured him. No one knew what Usaeil had done to Xaneth. It was a shock that he had survived at all.

But survive Xaneth had. The Reapers had been trying to make contact with Xaneth ever since—without any luck. He had shown up a couple of times, but no one had been able to get much from him. That's when Aisling left to search for Xaneth. She had been the first female Reaper among them, and she had been daunting even before she was a Reaper. Whatever urged her to find Xaneth must be important. Though Kyran suspected her heart might also be involved.

He hadn't spent much time with Xaneth, but he had liked the royal Fae. Xaneth had navigated both the Dark and Light Fae worlds easily—not something many could do. Both sets of Fae had trusted him, which was unheard of. Xaneth would be a good match for Aisling. But it all came down to what kind of Fae he was after Usaeil's torture. The last thing Kyran wanted Aisling to have to do was take Xaneth out.

Especially if she had feelings for him.

As for Balladyn…he was their newest Reaper and was still adjusting to his new life. Though Kyran had to admit that Balladyn was taking everything in stride. He had nothing to leave behind, unlike so many of them. That didn't mean Balladyn wasn't hurting.

Or lonely.

Kyran stopped and blinked. He'd been so lost in thought that he had no idea where he was. He heard some of his fellow Reapers around him, laughing and talking as they chose spots for their trees. Kyran lifted his head, trying to see the top of the mountains around him, but they were shrouded—no doubt by Erith to keep things secret.

He grinned, delight coursing through him once more. There would always be enemies to fight. But their family was strong. Their bonds unbreakable. It didn't matter if a Reaper was mated or not, they were family. And there was nothing family wouldn't do for each other. He suspected that Aisling would find that out soon enough. Balladyn, too.

Kyran pivoted and turned to retrace his steps. He focused on River and her personality. He thought of her favorite colors and the things that always made her eyes light up. She had a quirky nature that he hadn't really gotten to see until they came to live on Death's realm. In that safety, she had let her true self shine.

When he returned, he found that Cael had cut a winding path through the thick forest, wide enough for four people to walk side by side. Sitting against the snowbank on either side were paper lanterns that lit the way.

"What do you think?" he asked.

Kyran nodded. "River loves all kinds of lights like this. The way it shows the winding path is romantic."

"I thought so, too." Cael jerked his chin up ahead where

the path gradually inclined. "I found a clearing up ahead that would be nice for the large tree."

"Will you get that one?"

Cael bowed his head. "I'd be honored."

The path Cael chose made it so there could be decorated trees on either side. When he turned to tell the others, he found they had come to that same conclusion.

"We're going in order of when our mates arrived," Talin said with a wink. He then pointed to the other side of the path. "You're there."

Kyran glanced at Baylon, who was deep in thought with his tree. A look at Talin told Kyran that his friend was also engrossed. So were the other Reapers. He took a deep breath and walked to the spot where he wanted to put his tree for River. With just a thought, the twelve-foot green spruce appeared, drenched in tiny lights. He smiled as he thought of her favorite color—peacock green.

While River might be quirky, she was also traditional. He considered that as he brought in bronze and clear ornaments in all shapes and sizes, laying them out before him on the snow. He smiled and added a few actual peacock ornaments as well as feathers. Then he looked back at the tree. He thought back to how meticulous River was when she'd decorated their tree at home.

The ribbon had gone first. He used his magic to materialize it as well as drape it around the tree. Only then did he hang each ornament, one by one. At the top of the tree, he used the peacock feathers, making the tree nearly as colorful as the bird itself.

Kyran was pleased with himself at the finished product.

After one last look, he glanced around. He spotted a white tree with pale blue and silver decorations, a gold tree with navy ornaments, a green tree with blue, green, and gold plaid, a green tree with animal print everything, a flocked tree with pink lights and pink and white ornaments, and so many more.

He walked along the path, taking it all in. He listened to his friends' laughter and conversation, his heart overjoyed at what they were doing. The dinner was that night, but he could hardly wait. Was this what human children felt like on Christmas Eve? He wanted to go get River right then and show her everything. Kyran managed to hold off because he knew the impact of seeing all the lights from the path and the trees at night would be spectacular.

When he finally reached the end of the path, he stared at a grand tree over twenty feet tall. It was right that the path ended at Erith's tree. If it weren't for her, none of them would be here now.

He glanced to the side and saw Cael walking up. "This is nice."

"Too big?" Cael asked.

Kyran shook his head. "She's a fekking goddess. This isn't too big at all."

It wasn't long before the other Reapers joined them and surrounded the tree.

"Well?" Torin asked. "Who's decorating this one?"

Kyran looked around him. "We all are. This is for Erith. From all of us. It needs to be about her."

"Flowers," Eoghan stated.

Bradach grinned. "Sugared fruits and berries."

"Crystals," Fintan said.

With every suggestion, the Reapers began adding to the tree. There were flowers in a multitude of colors. The sugared berries and fruits gave the tree some sparkle, but it was the crystals that really brought out the clear lights of the tree.

Kyran held out his hands and thought of the custom ornament for him and River to add to the tree. A box, wrapped with a simple bow, appeared in his hands. He set it beneath the lowest branches and stepped back to look at Erith's tree before turning and looking at the others.

"The girls are going to love this," Baylon said.

Rordan sighed softly. "I just wish Aisling could be here."

"She's doing what she has to do," Balladyn said.

Everyone looked at him, but he said nothing more.

"It's time to get back to our houses and get ready," Daire said.

Rordan's eyes crinkled as he handed Breac to Kyran. "I wonder what Fianna is going to wear. See you all later."

Just as Kyran was about to teleport out, he saw Balladyn walking back down the path a ways to stand before a tree. Kyran wasn't the only one to remain. Cael was there, as well.

"Go," Kyran told Cael. "I've got this."

Once Cael was gone, Kyran made his way to Balladyn. The slim tree he stood before was only seven feet tall but heavily flocked with snow, weighing the limbs down. There were a few white ornaments among the snow and lights and pinecones. The tree was simple.

"I don't need to have a mate to craft a tree." Balladyn turned his head, his eyes meeting Kyran's. "I told you that you didn't need to worry about me."

"You're family. We worry. It's what we do."

Balladyn's lips curved slightly. "This is the first time in my life that I feel like I truly belong somewhere."

"Because you do, brother." Kyran clapped him on the back. "You're welcome to come to the house and arrive with us for dinner. I know I wouldn't turn down an extra pair of hands with Breac."

Kyran waited as Balladyn searched his face. He hoped Balladyn didn't hear the lie. Or that if he did, he realized it was coming from a good place.

Balladyn bowed his head. "I'd be honored."

"Come, then. River will be ecstatic to have you there. Although," he said with a frown, "she's probably going to try to tell you what to wear."

Balladyn snorted. "She only does that to you because you have no taste."

"What?" Kyran asked, his mouth gaping as Balladyn teleported away. Kyran then laughed and jumped to his house.

CHAPTER FIVE

"Bloody hell, woman."

River smiled at the husky sound of Kyran's voice behind her. She lifted her gaze to the mirror and met his red eyes. They burned with desire, causing her stomach to flutter with excitement…and pleasure.

"You like it?" she asked.

He slowly made his way to her, coming up behind her with his eyes lowered. He placed his hands on the shimmery gray fabric, lingering on her waist for a moment before lowering to her hips. His left hand moved around to the slit over her left thigh and parted the skirt.

His gaze lifted, meeting hers. He held the connection as he lowered his mouth and placed a kiss on her bare shoulder. "You know how I love when your shoulders are bare."

It was exactly why she had chosen this off-the-shoulder design. The skirt fell to just above her ankles, and the three-quarter-length sleeves would help to keep her warm. But she really loved how the dress accentuated her waist with the long slit giving it a sexy vibe.

"Minx," he whispered and kissed her shoulder once more.

River turned in his arms. She was happy that she had left her hair down when he lifted a long, dark strand and played with the ends. "Just for you, sweetheart."

"We can be late to the dinner, right?"

"Absolutely not," she said with a laugh.

His eyes burned with desire. "Tonight, then."

"You bet your ass," she said as she pulled his head down for a kiss. "Now. Let me look at you."

She eyed his burgundy velvet blazer with its charcoal gray lapels. He'd paired it with a dress shirt of the same color and black slacks. In his jacket pocket rested a burgundy, black, and gray square.

"Perfect," River said as she smoothed her hands over his shoulders.

He turned her so they could look at themselves side by side in the mirror. "I'm glad I asked what color you were wearing."

"Me, too," she said, turning her head to him.

He winked at her. "I left Breac with Balladyn. I'd better go check on them. We'll leave whenever you're ready."

River touched her ears to make sure the silver dangle earrings were in place. "I'm ready."

Kyran held out his arm for her. She took it, and they walked out of their room together and then down the stairs. They found Breac standing next to Balladyn, who sat on the sofa. Breac was busy giving Balladyn all of his toys. Kyran halted. River glanced at her mate to see his shock. She took a closer look at Balladyn and saw that there was a softness about his face that she hadn't seen before. He looked relaxed. And his laughter surprised both of them.

"Mummy," Breac cried when he saw her.

He moved too fast and tripped over Balladyn's feet. The Reaper quickly grabbed him and set the boy upright so he could continue to River. She lifted Breac into her arms and smiled.

"I figured you had enough to take care of," Kyran said when she noticed that their son was already dressed.

Breac was dressed exactly like Kyran but in a black blazer and burgundy shirt. River placed a kiss on her son's cheek. "You look as handsome as your father."

River then turned to Balladyn to find him in a thick, red, V-neck sweater with a white button-down beneath, and a deep brown and red tweed blazer that he'd paired with black jeans. He had his long hair pulled into a queue at his neck.

"How lucky am I to arrive with three such handsome men?" River said as she smiled at Balladyn.

He inclined his head to her, a smile playing about his lips.

"But I'm the handsomest, right?" Kyran said as he took Breac from her.

River flashed a knowing grin to Balladyn before turning to her mate. "Without a doubt, sweetheart."

"Are we ready?" Kyran asked excitedly.

River licked her lips, suddenly nervous.

"It's going to be great," Balladyn said into the silence.

She turned her gaze to him. "Thanks."

Kyran cleared his throat. "I'll be happy to take us there, baby, but you have to tell me where we're going."

"Oh," she said with a laugh and took both his hand and Balladyn's so they could all go together. "The top of the mountain. Talin said you'd know the one."

"Ah," Kyran said.

In the next instant, they were on the mountain with snow flurries dancing in the air. Breac erupted in laughter and tried to catch them. River wrapped her arms around herself to keep warm.

"River," Kyran said in awe as he looked around at the structure and landscaping. "You did all of this?"

Balladyn released her hand and took Breac from Kyran. "This is breathtaking. You and Kyran enjoy it while Breac and I go explore the rest."

Kyran didn't even seem to realize that Balladyn had taken their son. He was still looking around at everything. River hadn't seen some of it because Erith had wanted to keep it a surprise.

Outside of the structure, on either side of the double doors, were three, four-foot fir trees swathed with white lights and a smattering of red jingle bells for color. Between each tree were clumps of ten or twelve-foot-tall sticks of lights.

"If this is what it looks like out here, I can't wait to see the inside," Kyran told her.

She took his hand with a smile and led him through the doors. They weren't the first to arrive. Several couples were already there milling about. River halted them just inside and let Kyran look his fill. His lips were upturned, his eyes bright with excitement. Only the soft glow of candles and the festive lights illuminated the inside. The chandelier above them had been dimmed, as well. The tree looked beautiful in the back corner. The other three corners held stunning arrays of red, white, and pink flowers with lights strung through the arrangements.

"Baby, this is…I don't have the words," Kyran said as he looked down at her.

She tugged him after her to one of the side tables laden with various drinks such as eggnog martinis, sangria, and cranberry mojitos. She picked up a blackberry ombre sparkle cocktail with blackberries in a simple syrup at the bottom, champagne, and a sprig of rosemary for garnish. No surprise to her, Kyran chose a smoked cherry Old Fashioned. They clinked their glasses together and took a drink.

"Show me the rest," he urged.

River didn't need to be told twice. She pointed out the dessert tables laden with so many scrumptious treats she could barely believe it. River had her eye on the strawberry and vanilla macaron trifles in individual glasses. She laughed when Kyran's eyes lingered on the decadent chocolate layer cake.

He paused to look at the garlands strung around the room, pointing out different ornaments. They had been through so much, but she and Kyran had never paused to celebrate like this. Not at something the Reapers had done for themselves. Yes, they had been at Dreagan, but that wasn't their party. It was the Dragon Kings'. And while they'd had a grand time, tonight was all about the Reapers.

River's heart swelled as she glanced around to see other Reapers just as engrossed as Kyran. They weren't simply placating their mates, either. There was genuine happiness on their faces.

They were just turning the corner to the other set of double doors that led outside. "Not yet," River hastily turned Kyran so he wouldn't see what awaited them outside.

He chuckled but said nothing. His feet halted, however, when he saw the tree. Kyran let out a low whistle, and River's chest puffed up with pride. This season had always been one of her favorites, but this was a first for them—and it meant so much more.

"Babe," he whispered in awe.

Her eyes raked over the tall tree of white, gold, and red with its white lights. "It was a group effort."

"It's stunning."

"There's more," she said with a smile and tugged him onward to the tables of food.

They found Balladyn and Breac at the hors d'oeuvres table. The former King of the Dark held their son and let him choose what he wanted to sample before Balladyn handed it to him. River's eyes teared at the sight of Balladyn alone.

"Don't cry for him," Kyran whispered. "He promised me he was all right."

She turned her head to her mate. "But he's alone."

"Sometimes, that's for the best. We're all looking out for him. Don't worry."

She sniffed and nodded. When Breac saw them, he flashed a smile and waved but was content to remain with Balladyn.

"Besides," Kyran said, "it looks like our son has chosen him as date tonight."

River brought Kyran closer to the tables as they looked their fill at the delicious array before them. They spent several minutes simply inhaling all the amazing scents that awaited them. When Kyran's stomach rumbled, she turned him around to see the table.

A thick length of white tulle ran down the middle of the table to puddle on either end. There were no chairs at the end of the table strictly for that purpose. Beneath the tulle were strands of fairy lights. White tapers had been set every few feet down the middle of the table. One-inch-thick tree limbs held the votive candles placed between the tapers. Winding through the candles were sprigs of rosemary connected to look like one long runner. Added to the rosemary were sticks of cinnamon, as well as oranges with cloves stuck in them.

Each place setting was white with scalloped edges. Atop each plate were three candy canes tied together with a bow, each with a place card so everyone knew where to sit. The utensils were gold, and the red napkins added an extra pop.

"Wow," Kyran whispered, awe in his voice.

"You might have missed the view through the windows with everything else there was to see."

He chuckled and nodded. "I did at that."

"Then let me show you."

River pulled him toward the rear of the building. She opened the doors, and they stepped outside. More of the lighted sticks had been placed strategically around the seating area and along the edge of the mountain. Fur blankets awaited them on the sofas while a fire danced in the glass of the firepit.

She turned to glance inside, and that's when River saw the horizontal sticks on the outside of the building that held round, gold and white ornaments suspended from various lengths of red ribbon. There were also tall glass cylinders filled with fairy lights that mingled amid pinecones at the edge of the curved sofas.

"Is it everything you wanted?" Kyran asked as he wrapped an arm around her.

"That and more." She looked up at him.

He raised his brows. "This view is stunning. The snow does make it feel more like the season. I can't decide which area I like more."

She laughed and leaned her head against him. "We have all night to use it however you'd like."

"I think, right now, I want to just stand here with you and look at the stars."

River snuggled against him for warmth. "I like the sound of that."

The atmosphere was truly beyond anything Erith had expected. The only other party she had to compare it to was the one at Dreagan. Call her biased, but this one was truly outstanding. They sat around the table, laughing and talking. Most of the food was gone with a few still munching on desserts. Stories were being told, with tears of laughter following.

Erith's cheeks hurt from smiling so much. But she wouldn't change it for anything.

Still, she couldn't help but think back to the time when she had been totally alone. When she had watched other beings on realms, yearning for a family and somewhere to belong. Now, she had it—and she would do anything to protect those in her family.

The warmth of Cael's gaze drew her attention. They shared a smile before he lowered his eyes to the child in her arms. Breac had happily moved from person to person throughout the night. He had stayed the longest with Balladyn, as if the child understood that her newest Reaper might be the one with the most scars—and the one who needed extra love.

Breac had landed in her lap about twenty minutes ago, his fingers sticky from something she didn't want to guess at. After she had cleaned his hands and mouth, he had leaned back against her, listening to everyone. He had laughed when she had and tipped his head to the side to look up at her a few times. Then, he had turned around in her lap and wrapped his arms around her neck while resting his head on her shoulder. Within seconds, his breathing evened into sleep.

The last time she'd held a child had been Constantine and Rhi's twins. Eurwen and Brandr might have lived on her realm for a brief period, but they had left a lasting impression. It had been difficult for her to let them go their own way, but they had a destiny that was separate from her. That didn't mean she didn't miss them.

"You look good with a child in your arms," Cael said.

She pressed her cheek to the top of Breac's head. "I admit, I enjoy holding him."

Erith didn't say more. She and Cael had had a few brief conversations about having children. She wasn't sure if she could, but she wanted to find out. Yet, her duties and the constant enemies that seemed to crawl out of the woodwork kept her from giving in to her heart's desire. She kept telling herself that she had more than she ever thought possible. She had a family.

And she had Cael.

He covered her hand with his, one side of his lips lifting in a crooked smile. "We have eternity. It doesn't have to be now. When it's right, you'll know."

"And if it isn't ever right?"

He shrugged indifferently before glancing down the table. "I suspect we'll have other children to hold. They may not be ours, but they'll be a part of our family."

She smiled, her heart melting. There were many reasons she had fallen in love with Cael, but he had a knack for seeing her as no one else did. He understood her. Accepted her. Breac might have been a surprise for everyone, but she wasn't blind. She saw the longing in the females' eyes, and many of the males', too.

Erith pulled her gaze from Cael's and returned it to the table. She looked at each Reaper and their mate, recalling their stories and how they had come together. Their greatest foe yet was out there—the Fae Others. They wanted to destroy not just the Reapers but also her. They had tremendous power that Erith wouldn't underestimate. She had made that mistake in her past, and it had nearly cost Cael and her their lives.

She had vowed to never let that happen again, and she would hold to that.

Erith laughed at a story Jordyn was telling about Baylon. She could remain there for hours, days. River had been right. They *had* needed revelry. The party had taken the worry from them, at least for a few hours. The tension had left them all, and smiles were more readily visible. Love was in abundance.

Some didn't like her or the Reapers. It was because they threatened power that others clamored for. It was why Erith had insisted that no one know about the Reapers. If any Fae found out, she had ruthlessly cut them down. Because she had foreseen something like this happening. It was in the Fae's nature to want to gain and use power by either betrayal or blackmail. Erith had never wanted her Reapers put into that kind of predicament. She didn't enjoy the steps she'd had to take over the eons, but someone had to take them.

Now, despite everything she had done, the Reapers had been discovered and were being targeted. A plan had begun to form in Erith's mind for weeks now. It was risky and dangerous, but if it worked, it could give them back the ground they had lost to the Others. She was willing to take the chance for her family.

"Enjoy the night," Cael whispered in her ear. He placed a kissed on her cheek, his lips lingering for a moment.

She looked at him to find his eyes following his hand to her thigh and the black satin column dress she had chosen. When he saw her come out in the form-fitting outfit earlier, he had strode to her, lifted her, and claimed her mouth in a fiery kiss.

Erith didn't care that he had ripped her gown or messed up her hair in his hunger to sink inside her body. Afterward, she had simply fixed herself. Then, when they arrived at the mountaintop, she had seen the fire in his eyes once more.

She had taken his hand and pulled him into the woods where they gave in to their desires once more. Erith grinned because she knew her dress would likely be ripped for a third time later tonight. And she didn't care. How could she when the love of her life stirred such emotions within her?

Cael's hand halted when River stood and tapped her glass with her fork to get everyone's attention. Cael winked at Erith, a promise of pleasure in his smile before he focused on River. Erith took a deep breath and did the same.

"First, I wanted to thank everyone for their help," River said. "I had a vision, but this turned out so much better."

There was a round of applause with Bradach whistling loudly with his fingers. Breac stirred in Erith's arms before settling back to sleep.

River's eyes were bright as she glanced at Kyran before saying to everyone, "The night isn't quite over. There are a few presents beneath the tree."

With just a thought, each present was set before its Reaper. Erith had made sure Balladyn had a gift, too.

"Before you open them," River hastily said, "I would like to make a toast to the one who made so much possible. Erith."

Erith's lips parted in surprise. Her eyes misted as she saw everyone lift their glasses to her. She blinked back tears as she took her flute and lifted it in reply.

A chorus of, "*Hear, hear*" followed.

As soon as the toast finished, Erith watched as some Reapers like Talin, Daire, and Cathal tore into their gifts like excited children, while others like Cael, Eoghan, and Balladyn carefully peeled back the wrapping as if they were afraid of breaking something.

Erith's attention was torn between Cael and Balladyn. Thankfully, the two were seated across the table from each other. Cael got his gift open first. He took out the crystal sphere with a purple flower suspended in the middle.

When his eyes met hers, she explained, "I picked that flower from the field where I first saw you in battle. I've kept it all these years because it's so special. It's part of where my love of purple comes from. From the very start, I knew you were special."

"You've had my heart from the first moment I saw your face," he told her. "I'll treasure this always."

She reached for his hand and squeezed.

Balladyn then lifted the lid from the box and pulled out the orb. On one side was him as the legendary Light Fae Warrior dressed in the uniform of a Queen's Guard. On the other, him when he was King of the Dark. It was only when he held it just right that the two converged into one picture, showing him the Fae he was now.

His gaze lifted to hers and held for a moment. Then he placed a hand over his heart and bowed his head in thanks. His eyes returned to the orb, staring at it. She hoped it would help him reconcile who he was. He had been the best of the best, and he had been the worst of the worst, but through it all, he had managed to hold onto the most precious parts of himself. He had the potential to do so much more. She wanted him to know that his coloring didn't define who he was. That was why she had offered him a position with her Reapers. Balladyn had more than earned it.

"I think he likes it," Cael whispered as he leaned close.

Erith hoped so. They were going to need Balladyn in the coming months. His past deeds could hold him back—or he could finally break free. She prayed it was the latter.

With the presents open and the others beginning to mill about the room, Erith thought they might be going outside to enjoy the stars and the light from the moon glowing off the snow-capped mountains.

"Wait," Cael said.

She frowned and realized that the Reapers were halting their mates, too.

Kyran got to his feet and rubbed his hands together. "I didn't realize until River told me how much she missed home that I've neglected a few things. We're Reapers, and we have many duties. Thanks to Erith, our family is safe here. But when we go off to fight, we leave them behind. We're so focused on our mission and taking out our enemies, that we forget who is here waiting for us." He looked down at River and took her hand. "Don't ever hesitate to remind me that you have needs that must be addressed. You wanting a party for all of us got me thinking."

"Always a dangerous thing," Fintan declared in a deadpan voice.

There were chuckles and laughter.

Kyran waited until that died down before he said, "The others and I have a surprise for all of you."

River's eyes widened. "Really?"

"What?" Erith asked as she swung her head to Cael.

Cael merely smiled and stood, holding out his hand.

"We're going as one!" Kyran called.

Everyone got to their feet and moved into a cluster away from the table. Balladyn took Breac from her, the child limp in his arms. Erith gave Cael a questioning look.

He shook his head. "You'll find out soon enough."

"Ready?" Kyran asked.

A round of agreement filled the air.

In the next instant, the group was out in the night, standing in a forest aglow with thousands of lights. Erith saw the winding path and the decorated trees, and the tears that she had been holding back threatened once more.

"Oh, Cael," she said.

"Happy holidays, my love," he replied as he took her hand and began leading her up the path.

CHAPTER SEVEN

River was so shocked that she couldn't move. How had she not known Kyran had been up to something? Because she had been so absorbed in getting the party ready. All the while, he and the others had been thinking about them.

She was vaguely aware of couples separating and walking the path. River saw the first tree and smiled. When she spotted the second, her feet came to a stop at the sight of the peacock feathers and the coloring of the tree. Her eyes took in the brightly painted peacocks, the ribbon, and the other beautiful ornaments.

"Merry Christmas, baby."

She jerked her head to Kyran. It took her a minute to realize what his bright smile meant. "You did this?"

"Aye. This is your tree," he said proudly.

She tried to halt the tears, but they fell onto her cheeks. "Oh, Kyran. It's beautiful." River threw her arms around him and held him tightly. "I love you so much."

"I love you, too."

River pulled back to look at the tree once more. She walked around it, finding new ornaments each time she searched. It was obvious that Kyran had put a lot of thought into each decoration. He had surprised her in the most special way, and she couldn't be happier.

Once she had looked her fill of her tree—which took some time because she couldn't tear her eyes from it—she and Kyran walked hand in hand along the path, looking at the other trees. Each Reaper had crafted a tree that matched their mate. It was such a unique element, and it touched all the women deeply. The cold air billowed past River's lips as she breathed, but she wasn't chilled. That was the great thing about being with someone with magic.

The path sloped gently upward. She tried to look ahead, but Kyran wouldn't let her. They wound through the forest, commenting on the decorations and the individualism of each tree. It wasn't until they got to the black fir with the red ornaments that she found herself crying once more.

"I miss Aisling."

Kyran wrapped an arm around her. "We all do. It's why we put a tree up for her."

"She'll make it back, won't she?"

"She'd bloody well better, or we'll go find her."

River nodded. "If anyone can accomplish her mission, it's Aisling."

They paused for a moment more before they turned to walk to the next tree and saw Balladyn standing off to the side, holding Breac. River realized that the flocked tree with pinecones was his. She was glad that he had done it. It wasn't as heavily decorated as many of the others, but it suited the Dark. Others might think him complex, but he wasn't. Not like some might expect.

His gaze met hers, and they shared a smile.

"I think Breac has a favorite uncle," she said.

Balladyn's grin widened. "That's good since he's my favorite nephew."

"Careful," Kyran warned with a smile. "He'll wrap you around his finger pretty quick."

"I think that ship has already sailed," Balladyn replied.

They laughed softly.

River walked to Balladyn and put her hand on his arm. "Let me know when you get tired of holding him."

"You two enjoy the night. Little Man and I will be just fine," Balladyn told her.

Kyran put his hand on her back. "Come on, sweetheart."

River walked away, but her eyes lingered on Balladyn and Breac until she had no choice but to face forward. "I love our big family. It might not be perfect, but it's ours. Good or bad, we stick together."

"I couldn't agree more."

She quite liked the lighted path among the tall trees of the forest. It was romantic and special, a moment she would never forget. River smiled up at Kyran. Just when she didn't think she could love him any more, he did something that made her heart melt all over again. There had been so many things that had to go just right for them to even meet. Many more for the love between them to blossom and grow. They were proof that some things were destined.

When the path ended, a massive tree drenched in flowers

caught her attention. She gasped because she knew the Reapers had done this for Erith.

"Erith?" River whispered because she was crying again and didn't want her voice to break.

Kyran nodded. They joined the growing group of Reapers and mates. Erith stood to River's left, tears falling unchecked down her face as Cael stood beside her with his arm around her.

"We're not quite done," Kyran whispered. "You'll each find a gift under there with your name. Look for the paper that matches your tree."

River was hesitant to walk forward, but the other mates joined her as soon as she did. She squatted and looked among the presents. Lifting the first one, she saw Breda's name and passed it down to the Fae. The mates shifted gifts until they each had theirs. River stood and took her box back to Kyran.

He nodded. "Open it."

She carefully unwrapped it to find a white velvet box inside. When she lifted the lid, she found a peacock ornament like the ones on her tree.

"It's to hang on Erith's tree."

River turned around and pointed toward the top near a cluster of amaryllis and white daisies. "There."

Kyran used his magic and hung the ornament just where she pointed.

It didn't take long for the other mates to suspend their ornaments on the tree. Erith's tears came quicker, but she wasn't the only one crying. Their family stood around the magnificent tree and everything it represented for them.

No one knew what would come tomorrow, but they had

this night. They reminded themselves and each other of their love and their bond. Like any family, they had their ups and downs, but they stuck together no matter what. Just as they would with whatever they had to face next.

My *FIERY* *Valentine*

A Dark Kings Special Valentine's Day Novella 

"Epic. Heartbreaking. Thrilling."
— #1 NYT Bestselling Author Rachel Van Dyken

DONNA GRANT

NEW YORK TIMES BESTSELLING AUTHOR

CHAPTER ONE

Dreagan

V opened his eyes to see the sun breaking over the mountains through his window. A smile immediately pulled at his lips. All the worries that had once weighed heavily upon him were gone. He turned his head and looked at his mate. Claire was curled on her side, facing him, one hand under her cheek and the other tucked against her. Her blond hair was spread out behind her against the deep gray sheets.

His heart swelled as he stared at her. She slept peacefully with her lips parted slightly. It still boggled his mind that such a woman could love him. Claire was everything to him, and he made sure that she knew it every day. He wanted to touch her face and feel the soft skin beneath his fingers, but he was loath to wake her. A Dragon King might not need sleep, but humans did.

A sound on the other side of the bed drew his attention. V

rose on his elbow to peer over Claire into the bassinet to see his daughter waking. V slid from the bed without waking his mate and hurried to Pearl. He scooped up his bairn, smiling as she gazed up at him with large blue eyes that mirrored his. The fine dusting of hair atop her tiny head was too faint to determine if she would have V's dark locks or Claire's fair ones. V couldn't care less. Pearl would be perfect no matter what coloring she had.

He carefully cradled the infant against him as she reached for his finger. Pearl was still young, but V already knew she far surpassed any other child ever born. He laughed softly to himself, thinking how Claire rolled her eyes every time he said that.

V carried Pearl to the rocking chair and lowered himself into it. He still had a difficult time believing that his child had been born. It wasn't that humans couldn't get pregnant from a King, but when two different species tried to procreate, things didn't usually work out. Most human women miscarried early on in their pregnancies. Only a handful carried a bairn to term—and none of those had ever lived.

Until Pearl.

V didn't want to think about how Usaeil, a Dark Fae, had used her magic to ensure that Claire became pregnant to hurt V and the rest of the Dragon Kings. For Claire's entire pregnancy, they had steeled themselves for a miscarriage. As the weeks and months passed and her belly grew, they began to fear that the babe would come—only to be stillborn.

He looked at the bed. Claire had done her best to handle the stress, but it had been too much—even for him. They had leaned on each other as well as the rest of their large family at Dreagan. And, somehow, they had gotten through each day.

However, V had sunk deeper and deeper into gloom as the day of Pearl's birth loomed. When they located the dragons that had once called Earth home, everyone rejoiced. Everyone, that is, except for him. He couldn't think of anything but how he and Claire would survive if their child were stillborn.

Constantine, King of Dragon Kings, was the one who'd suggested that V take Claire to Zora. The realm was similar to Earth. The one main difference being the dragons. Claire had been mesmerized by the sight of them, but V had been too focused on her to pay any attention. Con believed that the bairn might have a chance if it were born outside of Earth. And Claire had been up for anything. V hadn't wanted to refuse her, even though he hadn't held the same hope as his mate or Con.

When Claire went into labor, V had felt every pain that wracked her body. He was a Dragon King, a being with immeasurable power. And he'd never felt so helpless before. Or useless. Her labor had stretched for hours, and the sight of her losing strength was like a dull blade twisting slowly into his spine. He knew that something was wrong. Everyone did. But no one knew what to do.

Until Brandr, Con and Rhi's son, stepped forward and laid his hand on Claire's extended stomach. V still wasn't sure what had happened. One minute, Claire was screaming in pain, begging him to save their baby. And the next, Pearl was born.

V later learned from Brandr that Usaeil's magic—the same magic that had created Pearl—had been preventing the bairn's birth. Usaeil had meant for Pearl to die. Along with Claire. She might be mated to a Dragon King, bound to live as long as V did, but her child's death would have killed her in other ways. Whatever Brandr had done had saved Claire *and* Pearl. V knew that to the depths of his soul.

He owed Brandr a debt that could never be repaid.

"You're frowning again."

V blinked at the sound of Claire's voice and stirred. Then he met Claire's striking brown eyes. "Good morning, beautiful."

She shoved aside the covers and rose to shove her feet into slippers and put on her kimono robe. Claire tied it at her waist and walked to him. She leaned over and kissed him. "Good morning, handsome." She then looked down at Pearl and kissed her head softly. "Good morning, sweetheart."

When she straightened, Claire raised a brow. "Vlad."

He winced and lowered his eyes to Pearl. "I know that tone. Your mummy isna going to take my silence as an answer."

"No, I'm not."

V continued rocking Pearl. "I'm fine."

"We're safe, babe. Look at her. She's growing like a weed."

He chuckled. Claire was right. They were safe. At least, until Pearl got older. They had no idea what magic she might have. Would Pearl be able to shift into a dragon? The more pressing question was how would he ever keep track of his daughter in the huge manor? What if she fell down the stairs? Because that was inevitable, wasn't it? Or what if she decided to slide down the banister?

Then there was others' cruelty. Someone would inevitably hurt her. That couldn't happen. He wouldn't let it. Just as he wouldn't let any boys near her.

Ever.

"V," Claire said with a sigh.

He glanced up at her. "Is she safe? I mean, look at her. She can no' feed herself. She can no' stand, she can no' even sit up. She can no' walk, she—"

"No infant can."

"Dragons can."

Claire folded her arms over her chest. "She's half-dragon, half-human. We have no idea what to expect."

"My point exactly. I can no' believe I didna realize until now how many dangers are out in the world for humans. So many things can harm her."

"I turned out all right. Most mortals do."

"Most." He snorted. "How many doona? What if we say or do the wrong thing? Claire, we could really mess up our child."

Claire lowered her arms to her sides and sighed. "All new parents go through this."

"Are you?"

"Well, yes. Not quite so…"—she waved her hand in front of him—"dramatically as you."

He glared. He'd never been dramatic a day in his very long life. "Have you no' thought about how cruel people can be? How hurtful their words? I doona think I'll be able to handle anyone hurting her."

"It's going to happen, honey. We can't stop that. It's life. She has to learn."

"I know just how horrible life is," he stated. "Millions of years of it. I doona want that for her."

Claire squatted down beside him and put a hand on his arm. "That's normal. We can't—and *won't*—coddle her, though. We're going to teach her how to be a good person, how to make the right choices, and then we'll give her the freedom to make mistakes, get her heart broken, and learn."

"I bloody hell will no' let anyone break her heart. There will be no boys. I'll incinerate them with dragon fire."

Claire flattened her lips. "You're being dramatic again."

"Tell me the idea of a boy taking advantage of her, of ripping her heart out, doesna make you see red," V demanded.

She leaned forward and placed her lips on his before sitting back. "It does. More than you'll ever know. But that's all part of life. She has to know pain so when the right kind of love comes, she'll recognize it."

He parted his lips, ready with another response, when Claire added, "Just as I did."

All the words he'd been about to say vanished as he gazed at his mate. "You said that to trip me up."

"It's the truth. Though, I might have said it to make you think. We can't stop her from getting hurt. If we do, we'll only make things more difficult for her."

V blew out a breath and looked at Pearl. "I never realized how difficult being a parent is. How am I going to do this?"

"We'll do it together. Like we do everything."

He reached for her hand and covered hers with his. "Do I want to know how many men broke your heart?"

Claire smiled. "Nope."

"You doona plan on telling me how many hurt Pearl either, do you?"

"Nope," she said, still smiling.

He grunted. "That might be wise. I'll be hard-pressed no' to do them harm, and I suspect I willna be the only King who feels that way."

"With a manor full of uncles and aunts, you're probably right," she said with a chuckle.

"Speaking of the manor, I've been meaning to talk to you about something."

Pearl started to fuss. V rose and handed the bairn to Claire so she could feed Pearl. He waited until Claire had settled in the rocker before continuing.

"Our chambers are spacious, but Pearl will need her own room soon."

Claire met his gaze, her lips tightening at the corners. "Eventually."

It was his turn to quirk a brow. "You just told me we shouldna coddle her."

"That doesn't mean we kick her out of our bedroom now."

"I never said she was leaving now. And there will be no kicking. You know I'm right about her needing her own space, though."

Claire frowned as she looked at Pearl. "I know. It's just…"

He nodded, fully understanding. "I know, love."

They sat in silence for a long while. It was Claire who finally spoke. "The rooms around us are taken. I don't feel right asking anyone to move."

"We can move. You could decorate both chambers as you want."

She smiled. "I like your taste. I want to keep that in our room. But I would like to decorate Pearl's."

"Whatever you want. But before you set your heart on that, there are a few other options."

Her blond brows snapped together. "Really?"

"Con spoke with me before we left Zora to return to Dreagan. It seems he and Rhi thought about what we'd need before we did."

"I couldn't think of a baby's room or what I needed. I couldn't let myself hope," Claire said in a soft voice.

He pulled a chair up so he could sit and face her. "Neither of us dared to believe we'd have our child. We're past that now."

"Weren't you just the one frowning about that when I woke?"

"We were talking about living options," he said in hopes of returning to the subject.

She flattened her lips and gave him a side look. "Mm-hmm."

"Con said we can convert the two rooms I spoke about in the manor into a two-bedroom flat. The second option is we can add onto the manor. I can take you later and show you the area. The third option is for us to build our own place. Dreagan is sixty-thousand acres. We have plenty of space to do it."

"If we build, we wouldn't be with the others. You've always been at Dreagan."

"You mean when I wasna in my mountain?" He shrugged. "Things change. We Dragon Kings have always adapted."

Claire shifted Pearl to place her on her shoulder and lightly pat her on the back. "Which do you prefer?"

"I'll be happy anywhere with you. It doesna matter to me. I'd rather *you* be happy."

She winked at him. "I am. Blissfully so. I don't want this just to be my decision. We do this together."

Claire settled Pearl in the bassinet, lingering for a moment to stare in wonder at the bundle that she and V had made. Her mobile dinged. Claire reached for it and saw that it was a text from Sophie. The two had been friends for many years. It had begun with Claire working with Sophie at the hospital, but when Sophie became mated to her own Dragon King and opened a medical clinic near Dreagan, Claire had followed to work alongside her.

Everyone at Dreagan had begun texting Claire first before they showed up at her door. She appreciated their efforts to give V and her some alone-time with Pearl. Sophie's usual morning text check-in filled the screen. Claire couldn't help but smile as she sent off a quick reply, letting her friend know she was good.

With Pearl asleep once more, Claire took the opportunity to do yoga before walking to the bathroom with the baby monitor for a shower. Once she got the water going, she turned to the side and looked at herself in the mirror. She had gotten so used to seeing herself pregnant that the person looking back at her now seemed almost alien.

She laughed at her thoughts and moved beneath the spray. Every few seconds, she poked her head out to look at the baby monitor on the counter to make sure that Pearl was all right. V had left for a few hours to take care of some Dreagan business. They were settling into a routine of sorts. It would change frequently as Pearl grew, but they had the freedom to make adjustments as needed.

One thing Claire hadn't thought about was her job as a nurse for Sophie. She loved her work, though she hadn't been to the clinic in a few months due to the pregnancy. Sophie hadn't asked if she would return. V hadn't brought it up either. Plenty of others at Dreagan wouldn't hesitate to watch Pearl if it came to it. But was that what she wanted?

Claire finished her shower and stepped out with her hair wrapped in a towel. It had been some time since she had done much to pamper herself. Her hair was long and in need of a trim. She would love to get a manicure, and possibly a pedicure. Even a facial sounded delightful.

Fear and worry during the pregnancy had kept her cocooned at Dreagan with V. She leaned out of the bathroom to check on Pearl. Just because her daughter had been born didn't mean the apprehension stopped. It was just a different kind now. Much of what V had spoken of that morning were things she hadn't thought of yet. She was more anxious about making sure Pearl was fed correctly and as often as needed. There were just so many things for parents to fret over.

She shook her head and unwrapped the towel. Wet, blond

locks fell heavily against her shoulders. She really wanted a trim. Maybe she should take an hour and go and have that done. Her decision made, she picked up her phone to call V when she saw the date: February 14.

"Valentine's Day?" she murmured in shock.

Claire slowly lowered the phone as she tried to think of something to do for the occasion. It was the day of love, after all. She had leaned so heavily on V for the entirety of her pregnancy that she wanted to do something special for him.

A slow smile curved her lips as an idea formed. She wouldn't be able to do this alone, though. Fortunately for her, there was a manor full of people who could help. Claire hurried to dress, not bothering to dry her hair. She combed it and pulled it back in a low ponytail before sending a group text to the mates at Dreagan.

Within minutes, a soft knock sounded on the door. Claire opened it to see several smiling faces. They each greeted her before crowding around the bassinet. Not that she could blame them. She couldn't stop staring at Pearl, either.

"Okay, then," Cassie said as she turned to Claire, rubbing her hands together. The American's dark brown eyes glittered with excitement. "What can we do? Do you need a babysitter?"

Faith, another American, gasped. "Please, please say you need someone to watch that adorable bundle," she begged in her Texas twang.

Before Claire could answer, there was another knock. She motioned the next group in, looking at the women who weren't only friends but also sisters. So many faces stared eagerly back at her. The only two missing were Sophie, who was at the clinic, and Rhi, who was on Zora with Con and the other Dragon Kings.

"Yes," she told Cassie and Faith. "I am going to need someone to watch Pearl."

Darcy chuckled, flicking back her auburn curls. "That isn't going to be an issue."

Claire wrinkled her nose. "It might be. I realized what today is, and I wanted to do something for V. Just the two of us."

"Anson and I already decided to have a quiet evening," Devon replied in her British accent. "It wouldn't be a problem for us."

Denae, another Texan, said, "Include us in that."

"Us, too."

"Yeah. Us, too."

More chimed in. Claire found her eyes watering. She hastily looked away. Their family at Dreagan might be big—and growing with the addition of Jeyra and Tamlyn—but they were always there for each other. Always.

"Thank you," she said and sniffed.

Alexandra rubbed her hand along Claire's back. The American smiled brightly. "Anything you, V, and Pearl need. Perhaps planning for tonight?"

"Yes," Claire said, louder than she'd intended. She winced and listened for Pearl, but her daughter still slept peacefully. "I need...well, everything."

Shara winked before replying, her voice lilting with her Irish accent as she said, "There are plenty of us here with magic. We can get whatever you need."

"Absolutely," Eilish said in her mix of American and Irish accents. "Where would you like to start?"

Claire thought about that for a moment. "I'd love to get my hair trimmed and styled."

"Include me in that," Sabina chimed in. The Romanian lifted her curly, dark locks and glared at her ends.

Eilish raised her hand and flashed the silver finger rings that allowed her to teleport. "Easy. Would you like to add any other pampering?"

"Mani/pedis," Iona said in her Scottish brogue.

There were nods of agreement from everyone.

Gemma elbowed Kinsey as she said, "Kins and I were just talking about facials. You just had a baby, Claire. Not to mention the months leading up to it and all the stress that went with it. Pamper yourself."

"I was thinking about a facial," Claire said. "But that might be too much for one day."

Noreen rolled her crimson Dark Fae eyes. "It's never too much. We can make a day of it. Besides, don't you need something to wear?"

"Of course, she does," Annita replied. The Greek waggled her dark eyebrows. "A new outfit is the perfect accent."

Gianna tucked a strand of red hair behind her ear and asked, "What about tonight? What are your plans with V?"

Claire lifted her brows. "It's going to take more magic."

"Good thing we have a couple of Fae as well as some Druids here," Jane replied with a grin.

Eilish stepped forward. "Let's get started, then."

Before Claire could respond, V's large frame filled the open doorway to their bedroom. He looked around the room until he caught sight of Claire. "Apologies, ladies. Did I interrupt something?"

"We were going to take Claire for some pampering," Lily said, her cultured British accent filling the silence.

V's ice-blue eyes crinkled at the corners as he slowly smiled. "I think that's a wonderful idea."

Claire walked to him as he leaned down to kiss her hello. "You don't mind?"

"Of course, not. Go, love. I'm glad I came back early."

"Me, too."

Claire didn't have time to say more as Noreen came up beside her and said, "We'll be back later."

Before she knew it, Claire was at a spa. She didn't bother to question how any of her sisters with magic knew which one to go to that would have openings. It was just something she'd learned to accept as a Dragon King's mate.

Not long after, she was in a room, getting a facial. After that came a luxurious ninety-minute massage, followed by a manicure and pedicure. She was so relaxed, she probably could've floated back to Dreagan.

Sophie arrived at the restaurant for lunch after she had seen to her patients. The meal was fun with lots of laughter. Soon, it would be on to shopping. Claire wasn't horrible at the pastime, but others like Lily and Alexandra had been gifted with skills that surpassed the average person's aptitude for style.

"What look are you going for?" Lily asked.

Claire shrugged as everyone looked at her. "Sexy. Yeah, I want to be sexy again."

"Exactly what I was going to say. Go with sexy," Rachel said before the American finished the last of her wine.

Lily caught Claire's eye. "I have an idea."

In short order, they were in a department store. Claire happily waited in a dressing room as Lily, Alexandra, Gianna, and several others brought in outfits. Claire tried each of them on. She had been wearing nothing but sweats and yoga pants since they'd returned from Zora. Claire didn't expect to fit back into her pre-pregnancy clothes right away, but she also wasn't ready to find out they still didn't fit. Her friends had already thought ahead, though.

She liked a couple of the dresses, but when she put on the white, V-neck, off-the-shoulder, wrap sweater dress that fell just above her knees, she knew it was the one. The minute she saw herself, she fell in love. It accentuated her breasts while the belt showed off her waist.

Claire came out of the dressing room. "This is it!"

Nods of agreement followed before they whisked her away to where Lily had already picked out a pair of suede, over-the-knee boots in a nude color. When Claire looked in the mirror at the completed outfit, her excitement grew. She met Sophie's gaze in the mirror.

"It's perfect," her best friend said with a smile. "You look beautiful, and you're going to knock V off his feet."

With her purchases paid for and bagged, her next stop was the salon for a much-needed trim and style.

Only then did she send V a text that said:

Already have babysitters in place. We're having a night for ourselves. Be ready.

She giggled, barely able to contain her excitement for what

she had in store. Just as she was about to discuss her plan, she looked around at her sisters. Yes, the manor could be loud and crowded at times. While many of the Kings were mated, and everyone enjoyed their privacy, there were also movie nights, Sunday dinners, game nights, and so many other fun things.

Did she want to move away from that? They were a family. Not by blood, but that didn't matter. Pearl should grow up with that. She would still have some of that if Claire and V moved somewhere on the estate, but it wouldn't be the same.

The family at Dreagan had been through so much over the last handful of years. A special bond had formed between all of them. The Kings had that after the war with the humans when the dragons were sent away, but the mates had found it little by little whenever danger came too close, and they had to defend themselves and each other.

It was the kind of family that would always be there. The kind that would never turn their backs on one another. The kind of family that Claire wanted her daughter to grow up in. Besides, Claire suspected that she would need all the help she could get with a half-human, half-dragon baby with who-knew-what kind of magic.

CHAPTER THREE

The instant Claire left with the other mates, V opened the telepathic link that all dragons had and called to Nikolai and Sebastian. *"Do you have an update?"*

A loud huff sounded before Nikolai said, *"You showed us a picture on social media two seconds before you left."*

"It's coming along," Sebastian said with a laugh. *"It would be better if you were here. Can you get away?"*

"Claire just left with all the other mates. I suspect she'll be gone for some time."

There was a beat of silence before Nikolai asked, *"You're no' going to fly with Pearl, are you?"*

"Why no'? She's half-dragon," Sebastian stated.

V could practically hear Nikolai roll his eyes before he said, *"We have no idea what magic Pearl will have. She may no' be able to shift or fly."*

"She may no', but I bet she'll love being flown around by

her da and all her uncles," Sebastian answered, a smile in his voice.

V stood over the crib. His daughter slept peacefully. *"I'll be there once Pearl wakes. Just keep looking at that picture on the Internet. I want it like that but different."*

"Och. You should get here soon," Sebastian replied. *"We'll do the best we can until then."*

V severed the link and looked around the room. He spent a few minutes tidying up. He could've used magic, but he chose to do it himself. The Kings didn't like to use magic unnecessarily. Though, there were times that called for it.

Magic had been a way of life for him. It was all he had ever known. On occasion, he wondered how humans fared without being able to call magic as dragons did. Dragons were powerful creatures. No other being on the realm could match them in magic. V didn't claim that dragons were the most powerful in the universe because he didn't know what was on other realms. Hell, they were still learning about the beings on Zora.

The half-dragons he knew could shift, though. Surely, that meant Pearl would be able to go from human to dragon and back. Those he knew who were dragon and other—Melisse, Brandr, and Eurwen—were also half-Fae. And had magic.

Some mortals could call magic, like the Druids. Claire actually had some distant connection to the Isle of Skye and the Druids there. While they knew that, she couldn't do magic herself.

V sighed. It didn't matter if his daughter had magic or could shift. He would love her no matter what. It was a miracle that she had been born at all. It was enough that he had her. Just when the worries from earlier began to creep up on him again, his daughter gurgled from the bassinet.

V made his way to her. He lifted her and bent to kiss her forehead when he smelled why she had woken. "All right, wee *yin*. I'll get you cleaned up."

Pearl watched him intently as he changed her nappy. When she was clean, he glanced outside to see the snow-capped mountains against the blue sky and realized he didn't have warm enough clothes for her—and no time to go shopping. Not if he wanted to have everything ready for Claire. V shrugged and used his magic to ensure that Pearl was bundled properly before carrying her from the room. No sooner had he stepped out the door than he saw Kiril in the hallway.

"Going somewhere?" the King of Burnt Oranges asked with a raised brow.

V glanced down at his daughter, swaddled so only her chubby face could be seen. "Do you no' think she'll be warm enough?"

"It's February. In the Highlands. We get the most snow this month. Humans find that cold."

V blew out a breath. He didn't know if Pearl was chilled, but it was better to be safe than sorry. The skies had been clear that morning, but there was always a chance of rain. Especially mixed with snow. Perhaps taking Pearl wasn't a good idea.

"What's going on?"

V looked into Kiril's shamrock-green eyes. "I'm giving Claire a surprise tonight. Bast and Nikolai are working on it for me."

Kiril held out his hands and motioned with his fingers.

"Give me Pearl. You go to Bast and Nikolai. I have no' had more than a second alone with this precious bean since the three of you returned from Zora."

"Bean?" V asked with a frown.

Kiril shrugged. "You have a problem with bean?"

V opened his mouth but couldn't come up with anything. Finally, he shook his head.

"Hand over the wee bean and be on your way," Kiril said with an eager smile.

V grudgingly handed Pearl to Kiril. "Do you even know what to do with a bairn?"

"I'm no' an idiot."

"Have you changed a nappy?"

Kiril gave him a flat look. "How hard can it be?"

V choked back his laugh as he imagined just what Kiril would find himself elbow-deep in. "Right. How hard can it be?"

"Do I need to walk her?"

"She's no' a dog," V snapped, thinking he might be better finding someone else.

Kiril rolled his eyes. "I was joking."

V studied him, unsure if Kiril was jesting or not. "There's breast milk in the fridge in my room. It needs to be heated—"

"I know, I know. Shara has been talking nonstop about everything so we would be prepared when we got to babysit. I'll test it on the inside of my wrist and make sure it isna too hot." Kiril then lifted Pearl up to his face and said in a baby voice, "Is that no' right, my precious bean?"

To V's horror, his daughter grinned. He told himself it was just gas. That was the only reason she would smile at that name and the high-pitched voice he hoped never to hear Kiril use again. "I willna be long."

"Pearl couldna be in safer hands," Kiril said as he tucked her against him.

V wondered if Claire would have handed their daughter over as he had.

A gasp sounded behind him, then V heard Warrick ask, "Are you leaving, V? Do we get to look after the wee biscuit?"

"See," Kiril said with raised brows. "Bean is so much better."

V looked at the ceiling and shook his head. There would, no doubt, be a hundred different nicknames for Pearl. He knew his brethren. It would be a competition for which ones stuck, and which didn't. He was pretty sure *biscuit* would disappear quickly. At least it would if he had anything to say about it. Immediately followed by *bean*.

"I do have to head out for a bit," V said as War came up beside Kiril and made cooing noises at Pearl.

Of course, Pearl enjoyed the attention. V watched the two men, fearsome Dragon Kings, reduced to a pile of mush by his infant daughter. V had given Claire the decision of where they would live, and while he knew his small family needed their own space, he wanted to stay at the manor. He'd tried to tell himself that having a house on Dreagan wouldn't be that different, but it would. There would be no running into anyone in the hall. No large dinners or game nights.

Then again, it wasn't just Claire and him anymore. They had a daughter to think about now. Maybe it wouldn't be good for her to have everyone constantly surrounding her. Maybe that wouldn't be good for Claire or him, either.

Perhaps some space was best. It wouldn't change anything. They could still come to the manor for game nights—until Pearl got older and had homework or soccer or whatever she did.

V rubbed his forehead and realized that his friends were staring at him. "You try having a bairn and no' think about all the horrible stuff that could happen to them."

"She's in the safest place on the realm," Kiril pointed out.

War nodded. "Surrounded by the most powerful beings on the planet."

"It still doesna stop the worry. I'm beginning to think that it willna matter how old she is. I'll have new fears with every age."

Kiril chuckled. "No doubt, brother."

"We'll be fine here, just as soon as we get the biscuit out of this winter gear," War said.

Kiril snorted as they exchanged a look. "Way ahead of you. Can you believe V was going to take her out in this weather? You're sweltering. Aren't you, bean?"

V watched as the two walked into his chamber. He smiled as he heard them arguing over Pearl's nickname. V turned on his heel and headed for the stairs. He hurried down the steps and reached the bottom before lengthening his strides as he made his way to the conservatory and the secret door that led to the back of Dreagan Mountain.

He reached the enormous opening at the back and was about to shift when he heard his name. He glanced over his shoulder to see Arian striding toward him.

"Bast told me what he and Nikolai are doing. I thought I'd come and lend a hand," the King of Turquoises offered.

V nodded in agreement. "You doona have to get ready for tonight with Grace?"

"Oh, I had that taken care of weeks ago," he said with a smile crinkling his champagne-colored eyes. "I have a private dinner reserved. She bought a dress that she's no' worn yet, and I've seen her looking at it. This will give her that opportunity."

"She knows about it?"

"Grace knows we're going out. It coincided perfectly since she just turned in a book. She doesna know where we're going or that I've already placed the dress on the bed with a note. Along with dozens of roses throughout our room." Arian grinned and waggled his eyebrows.

V had to admit, that was a special night for them. "Nice."

"Come on," Arian said. "Let's get everything set up for you. How hard can it be to replicate the picture you showed Nikolai and Bast?"

V widened his eyes. "That's what I said!"

The two moved away and shifted. V glanced at Arian and met his black dragon eyes before running the few steps to the opening of the mountain and leaping into the air. V spread his wings and began to flap them as he climbed higher in the sky.

Dragons had once roamed freely on Earth. They had found a new home on Zora, but the Dragon Kings still hid themselves, flying only on Dreagan and mostly during storms or at night. For many, many years, Con had refused to let any of them fly during the day at all, but that rule had been relaxed some. The clout Con had was impressive, and he made sure to form friendships with those in power around the world. That, along with the invisible magical border that had been erected around Dreagan after the war with the humans, kept most people away. And magic alerted them if anyone broke through the barrier.

Of course, they'd had to adjust the border when they began making whisky and realized that humans would want to come to the distillery. There was also always the chance that someone with a drone would try to see onto Dreagan, but the Kings were ahead of things there, too, thanks to Ryder, their expert in everything technological.

V's mind silenced as he glided over the landscape. The rugged mountains capped with snow, the tree-lined glens, the magnificent waterfalls, rivers, and lochs. Dreagan had been their refuge, their haven. For a short time, V had even considered it his prison. Now, as it had been for countless centuries before—and would continue to be—it was his home.

The skies remained clear. V wondered if Arian had anything to do with that since he could control the weather. He didn't ask, though. Whatever the reason, he was happy to feel the sun on his copper scales.

When he spotted his mountain, a smile formed. He flew faster, eager to be there. V soared over it and looked down at the loch. He spotted Nikolai and Sebastian before he dipped his wing and swung around. As he approached, he began his descent. Once he landed and shifted, something heavy slapped against his face.

It was instinct to reach and grab for it. He blinked and looked down at the jeans in his hand. He looked up to find Bast, Arian, and Nikolai laughing. "Something funny?"

"We just didna want to see you naked," Nikolai replied.

V rolled his eyes and shoved his legs into the jeans. "You didna do the same to Arian."

"Because I made sure to call my clothes back to me before I landed."

"That's too much trouble," V grumbled. "There's nothing wrong with being naked."

Nikolai hit Bast in the stomach, his palm up. "I told you he would be naked. Pay up."

"I doona have it on me," Bast said with a frown. "I'll give it to you at the manor."

V used his magic to return his shoes and the sweater he'd worn earlier.

"So, when can Esther and I pick up Pearl for tonight?" Nikolai asked.

V should've known this would happen. His mind went blank as he tried to come up with something to say.

"You?" Bast said, scoffing. "It'll be Gianna and me, thank you verra much."

Arian snorted loudly. "You two really think either of you will get to watch the bairn?"

"That's the only reason you came out here to help," Nikolai stated.

Bast quirked a brow as he folded his arms across his chest. "I was in line first."

"What?" Nikolai and Arian said at the same time.

V shook his head, grinning as the three continued bickering over who would get to watch Pearl. He didn't have the heart to tell them that Claire had already set up a babysitter.

CHAPTER FOUR

Claire felt like a new woman when she returned to the manor. There was no sign of V. No doubt he was doing something at the distillery. That gave her more time to get ready. She had begun to get anxious when she realized what time it was. Her day with her sisters had gone by much quicker than she had expected.

It was also the longest she had been away from Pearl. She returned just in time for a feeding. Claire rocked her daughter, feelings of gratitude and love filling her. Not just for Pearl and V, but also the large family she had come into. Then there were her parents. Because of who she had given her heart to, she wasn't able to tell them anything about who V really was. They knew only that he was part owner of Dreagan whisky—which made her father especially happy since it was his favorite scotch.

There were times she wished she could tell her parents everything. During her pregnancy, she'd had to keep her real worries from her mother when she had always turned to her mum in times of need. But her parents were making the journey to see Pearl in a week. Claire could hardly wait. That was for another day, though. Tonight was for her and V.

"Your da is in for a surprise," she told Pearl. "I hope he likes what I have planned."

Claire wiped her daughter's mouth before shifting her onto her shoulder to burp her. After she got a rather loud one from Pearl, Claire continued rocking until Pearl drifted off to sleep once more.

Only then did Claire set about getting ready. She hoped V would stay away until she was clothed. She hung up her dress and got out the boots. Then she retrieved the new ivory lace bra and panty set. Only then did she remove her clothes and put on her robe to apply her makeup.

It was one of those rare occasions when the makeup went on perfectly—including her mascara, which *never* happened. She looked at herself in the mirror and smiled. All the tension and stress of the past nine months had been worked from her muscles—well, it might not be gone entirely, but it was definitely a start. She felt immeasurably better. The facial, haircut and style, along with the mani/pedi and spending time with her sisters, was just what she had needed.

Claire stood and removed her white kimono with its large navy flowers along the back and down one side and hung it on the inside of the closet door. Then she put on her new lingerie. Excitement raced through her. This was, for all intents and purposes, the first date she and V had been on in months, and she wanted to look her absolute best.

She carefully put on the sweater dress. Once she'd belted

it, she adjusted the shoulders so the deep neckline would draw her mate's eyes. Claire then put on the boots. She'd never worn over-the-knee boots, but she loved how they made her legs appear longer.

Claire pulled out the five-carat copper zircon necklace set in rose gold Con had gifted her when she mated V. Once the piece was in place, she put on the matching earrings V had given her at Christmas. She finished it off with a rose gold and copper bangle set. She was smoothing her hands down the dress with one last look at herself in the full-length mirror when the bedroom door opened. Her eyes met V's ice-blue ones in the mirror.

He stared at her for a long moment, letting his gaze move slowly down her body. His voice was deep and thick when he said, "You're more beautiful every time I look at you."

She wore a smile when she turned to him. It was her turn to see him, and he hadn't skimped. He wasn't in a kilt, which was her favorite thing to have him wear besides nothing, but she didn't care because he had a way of wearing clothing that made it look as if he had been born to wear it.

"No' enough?" he asked. "I can make it dressier."

Claire shook her head as she walked to him and ran her hand over the chocolate brown corduroy blazer with hints of bronze. The white dress shirt looked amazing beneath, along with a plaid vest of deep brown, cream, white, and black. He'd paired it all with dark denim, a deep brown belt, and matching shoes. "You are very handsome, husband."

His arm wrapped around her to drag her close as he brushed his lips over hers once, then twice before kissing her deeply. She sank against his body, letting his heat and love surround her. Only V could make her feel so appreciated and loved, so deeply and completely. It was in his actions, his words, and every decision he made.

He caressed his knuckles against her cheek as he ended the kiss. Then he looked down at her. "I doona think I tell you often enough how much I love you."

"You do," she said with a smile as she gave him a lingering kiss.

His lips compressed when she pulled back. "I should warn you that there is some bickering going on about who is going to watch our daughter."

"I've already taken care of it."

"Thank goodness. We're going to have to have some kind of spreadsheet or something to make sure we rotate."

"That bad, huh?"

He winced. "They're coming up with nicknames for Pearl. It's a competition."

Claire bit back a laugh as she stood in V's arms. "I like bean."

"No' you, too."

His shocked expression made a laugh bubble forth. "It's cute."

"For now. I doona think our daughter will appreciate being called *bean* when she's in her teens."

"Admit it. You like that your brethren are doing this."

V's lips split into a wide smile. "I do."

She shook her head, grinning. "You're impossible, but that's why I love you."

"Are you ready for the night to begin?"

"I was about to ask you the same thing."

His ice-blue eyes crinkled. "What have you planned?"

"It's time you found out."

She moved out of his arms long enough to pull on her long camel-colored coat before taking his hand and leading him to the door. Just as she'd expected, Cassie and Hal and Faith and Dmitri were waiting to take over the duty of watching Pearl for a few hours. After they made sure the two couples were all set, Claire led V down the three flights of stairs to the bottom floor.

She briefly met his quizzical gaze when she went out the side entrance instead of the garage. They wouldn't need a car for the night. The path that led to the distillery from the manor had been cleared so they weren't walking in snow.

"Claire?" V asked.

"Just wait," she told him as she led him past the buildings.

She didn't stop until she came to the warehouse. Once there, she watched his expression as they went inside. His lips parted in astonishment as he took in the lights hovering high above them for a romantic glow. A table for two had been set, complete with tapered candles. Soft music played in the background, and the aroma of food filled the air from a table off to the side stacked with a delicious array. A tall bucket of ice held a bottle of champagne.

"I wanted to give you a romantic dinner, but I couldn't find a place that was perfect. Then I remembered this," she said.

He squeezed her hand as he turned his head to her. "This is perfect."

"I was hoping you'd say that."

The warehouse was warm, so V helped her out of her coat and hung it on a peg near the door. He then walked her to the table and pulled out a chair for her. Next, he opened the champagne and filled their flutes before taking his seat.

V lifted his glass. "To our love that grows stronger every day."

"To our love," she replied, and they clinked glasses before drinking.

He looked around, smiling. "I never would've thought to use the warehouse."

"I probably wouldn't have, but it was last-minute, and this was the only place that wasn't being used tonight by the others. It helped that a large shipment of whisky went out two days ago."

V chuckled. "You amaze me every day, sweetheart."

Claire's eyes misted as she reached across the table for his hand. "We survived something we weren't meant to endure. On top of that, Pearl lived. I didn't think I could be happier than I was loving you, but our family is everything to me."

"It's because of your strength."

She shook her head. "I wouldn't have been able to do any of it without you."

"Nor I, you."

"It's why we make such a great team."

He brought her hand to his lips and kissed her knuckles. "One of the many reasons. I doona want to think of my life without you."

"You never have to worry about that. I've never been surer of anything than I am about my love for you."

"My life was complete when I found you. Pearl is a bonus I never imagined."

"A very loud, very messy bonus," Claire said with a laugh.

"Good thing we have so many aunts and uncles willing to help."

She nodded, thinking again about their family and their talk earlier that morning. Claire dabbed at the corners of her eyes with the napkin as emotions threatened to overtake her. "If we don't stop this talk, I'm going to start crying. Now, stay there. I can't wait for you to see what we have to eat."

She rose and started for the table when V was suddenly on his feet, his hand on her arm to stop her. He stood and turned her to face him. He gazed at her for a long moment before pulling her against him to simply hold her. She closed her eyes and held him tightly. He always knew what she needed. Whether it be words of encouragement, a kiss, or simply to be held, V was always there.

"I love you," she whispered.

He pulled back so he could see her face. "I love you."

Life would have been so much easier if she had known that her destiny had been written to mate a Dragon King. She wouldn't have spent so many years going out with the wrong men or enduring that horrible spell of online dating.

Then again, like she'd told V earlier, she'd had to date all the bad ones so she would know how wonderful it was to find her mate.

CHAPTER FIVE

Claire amazed and awed him. V fell more in love with her each day. It sounded impossible, but it was true.

The dinner was a complete surprise. He loved that she had gone to so much trouble for them to have a few hours alone together. And she didn't know about his surprise. Yet. V could barely contain himself. He wanted to whisk her away right then and show her, but he forced himself to remain quiet about it as they finished their meal and ate dessert.

"I think Keltan outdid himself this time," Claire said as she sat back in her chair.

V pushed aside his empty plate. "I think the best part was the company."

He loved the grin she shot him before she said, "I am pretty good, huh?"

V laughed at her teasing. "I was talking about me."

That made her nearly spit out her champagne. She covered her lips with her hand, her shoulders shaking as she fought to keep the liquid in her mouth. Finally, she swallowed. "I should've sprayed you."

They each laughed again before the sound tapered off. Claire sighed. "I guess it's time to return to Pearl."

"I wouldna say that."

Her blond brows snapped together. Then she shrugged. "I suppose we could remain a little longer."

V climbed to his feet and buttoned his jacket before holding out his hand. "I have another idea."

"Oh?" she asked as she slipped her hand into his and stood. "What might that be?"

"And spoil the surprise? I doona think so."

Her deep brown eyes grew round with excitement. "A surprise?"

"Do you actually think I would let this day pass without doing something?"

She wrinkled her nose. "I didn't realize what day it was until this morning. I've been otherwise occupied, so I wouldn't have blamed you had you done the same."

He pulled her to him and walked her to her coat, helping her into it. "Things have been a bit hectic. I doona expect that will change much."

"You're probably right. So, where are we going?"

V chuckled. "You'll have to wait and see."

"You know I can't handle surprises. I mean, I love them, but I have to know immediately what it is once I know I have a surprise. I don't like knowing it's out there and that I have to wait."

"It willna be too much longer now."

"How long are you thinking? Five minutes? Two?"

He didn't bother to answer as he pushed up the left sleeve of his jacket and shirt, revealing Ulrik's silver cuff imbued with Fae magic that would allow them to teleport. He had borrowed it so they could get back and forth from his mountain quickly in case there was an emergency with Pearl.

"V, is that Ulrik's brac—" she started as he touched it and teleported them to just outside his mountain. "—let? Yeah, I guess it is." Then her gaze caught the water. "Oh, look at that view."

He stood beside her as they gazed at the loch and the light of the rising moon reflecting off the perfectly still water. She leaned against him and rested her head on his shoulder. The silence around them was beautiful, broken only by an owl hooting in the distance and the flap of a bat's wings as it darted overhead.

"We should come here more," Claire whispered as if she were too afraid to speak louder. "Your mountain is beautiful."

He squeezed her against him and kissed the top of her head. "I always thought so."

"This is an amazing surprise. I don't think I've ever seen the loch look quite so spectacular."

"That isna your surprise."

Her head snapped up as she looked at him. "It isn't? Then what is?"

V could hold off no longer. He took her by the shoulders and gently turned her around to face where the yurt sat.

She sucked in a breath. Then, she said in a whisper full of awe, "Oh, wow."

V led her past the two chairs and the empty firepit to the entrance of the round, portable structure. He pushed back the heavy flap and waited for her to walk inside. The yurt was warm, thanks to a wood-burning stove. Tensions and suspensions held up the accordion roof, allowing for no center rod.

A low bed piled with neutral-colored blankets in various sizes and textures and enough pillows to match sat inside. Thick rugs in the same neutral tones as the blankets and pillows covered the ground. Hundreds of tiny lights filled the ceiling, creating a soft amber glow throughout the tent.

"Look at this," Claire said as she ran her hands through a solid white, faux fur blanket. "Oh, and this rug." She bent to feel its texture. Another blanket caught her attention. "This one is sooooo dreamy. Oh, but this one. And that one."

V stood back and smiled as his mate went through all the different blankets and pillows. Claire loved textures—the softer, the better. He had wanted to make sure she had all that she could possibly want.

She swung her head to him. "This is beyond anything. I don't even know what to say."

"You don't have to say anything."

"Maybe," she said with a shrug as she knelt on the bed. "But there is something I'd like to do."

He grinned when she beckoned him with a finger. V walked to her. "I can't imagine what that might be."

"Perhaps I should show you."

He wound his arms around her as his lips descended upon hers. The kiss was hungry, needy. His blood rushed straight to his cock that grew rigid, throbbing with need. He lowered his arms when Claire shoved his jacket off his shoulders, letting it fall to the floor.

"This would be the time to use your magic and make our clothes disappear," she said breathlessly between kisses.

V didn't hesitate to do as she asked. When they were skin to skin, he gently laid her back on the bed and covered her body with his. No matter how long he lived, no matter how many centuries they had together, he would always get the same thrill each time they made love. He ran his hands over her body. From her long legs and flared hips to the indent of her waist and the curves of her breasts, she was the most beautiful woman he'd ever laid eyes on. And she had given her heart to him.

Love and desire blended, creating a heady mixture. He took his time kissing her deeply before moving to her neck and her favorite spot right behind her ear that always drove her crazy. He grinned when her nails dug into his back. This was just the beginning of the night he had planned. By the time he finished with her, she wouldn't be able to move.

And neither would he.

V cupped her breast in one hand and massaged it before teasing the tiny bud until it pebbled. She arched her back.

"More," she pleaded.

He kissed down her stomach to the junction of her thighs as he settled between her legs. He looked up to find her head lifted as she watched him, desire darkening her soft brown eyes. He flashed her a grin before licking her.

The air whooshed from Claire's lungs as her head dropped onto the bed. With one touch, V had her begging for more. He had an uncanny knack for knowing what she wanted without her ever having to say a word.

She gasped, her eyes rolling back in her head as pleasure shot through her when he teased her clit. When she didn't think she could take any more, he began rolling her nipples between his thumbs. The onslaught was too much. Warmth rushed through her body as desire coiled low in her belly. She fisted her hands in the blankets as he drove her closer and closer to orgasm.

The force of the climax took her breath away. Waves of pleasure rolled through her, taking her higher. Tremors racked her body as she came back into awareness. That's when she felt V at her entrance. She opened her eyes and smiled as she reached for him.

Her lips parted in ecstasy when he filled her slowly, powerfully. He rocked his hips, grinding against her swollen clit. Claire wrapped her legs around him, pulling him even deeper.

V stilled and looked down at her. "I doona know how I ever lived without you."

"We each had a journey we had to walk before we were ready for each other."

"I love you so much."

She pulled him down for a kiss. "I love you more."

"I love you most," he said with a grin, punctuating his statement with a thrust of his hips.

Talking was forgotten as he began moving within her.

V pumped his hips, sliding in and out of Claire's wet heat. He loved seeing the bliss move across her face as he brought her to orgasm. He wanted at least three more from her before he gave in to his climax.

She flicked a nail over his nipple and grinned up at him. She knew what he was about. Claire had no problems with his plans, but she loved seeing if she could push him to the edge long before he wanted to go. She always won.

Just as she would tonight.

He kept his rhythm, driving deeper, harder. He knew by the change in her breathing that she was closer than he'd initially thought. A light sheen of sweat covered them both, allowing their bodies to glide against each other. The friction heightened their desire.

V was so intent on holding back his climax that he was surprised when Claire peaked for a second time. The feel of her body clenching around his cock broke his control. He buried himself deep and gave in to the pleasure.

His arms shook when he finally opened his eyes. V looked down to see Claire gazing at him drowsily. He pulled out of her and moved to his side. She rolled to face him as they interlaced their fingers and tangled their legs. They shared a soft smile.

"I have a confession," she said in a low voice.

He raised a brow. "What might that be?"

"I'm addicted to you."

V chuckled and shifted forward to kiss her. "That's a good thing since I'm entirely hooked on you."

"This night has been incredible. I love the yurt and all the little touches."

He winked at her. "I pay attention when my woman oohs and ahhs over things."

"I love texture. I can't help it. I'm keeping every blanket, pillow, and rug. They're utterly perfect."

It was the perfect time to ask about their living arrangements. V hesitated, wondering if they should leave the discussion for tomorrow. Tonight was about them.

"Can we talk about where we're going to live?" Claire asked.

He should've known that she would want to get it sorted immediately. "Of course. What are you thinking?"

"I was unsure this morning when you brought it up. I had begun to think that perhaps we needed some space as a family."

"I had that same thought."

She drew in a breath and wrinkled her nose. "Then I spent the day with everyone. It reminded me how they're willing to drop everything to help, even if it was just for me to get things ready for you and to pamper myself today. Maybe we can build a house away from the manor someday, but I'm not sure I'm ready for that now."

"I agree," he said with a smile.

Her eyes widened. "Really? That's good."

"That leaves two other choices. We add on to the manor, or we switch rooms. Shaw will be on Zora for the time being. He'll have no problem giving up his room so we can join with the empty one next to it and create our suite."

"It just feels wrong asking him to move."

"He offered."

She blinked in surprise. "Oh."

"We'd only be moving across and down the hall."

Claire bit her lip as she briefly lowered her gaze to their hands. "What is your preference?"

"There will be some construction no matter what. Marcas has already drawn up plans for all three ideas."

"Of course, he did," Claire said with a laugh. "He wouldn't pass up an opportunity to use his skills as an architect."

V winked at her. "He did design the manor."

"You never answered me. Which would you like better? An addition to the manor, or joining two chambers?"

"I'd be happy with either, but I'm leaning toward the two chambers."

A smile split her face. "Me, too."

"Then it's settled. We can move in as soon as you want. Shaw already took his things out, just in case."

"What if other mates become pregnant?" Claire asked. "It's all Sophie and Darius can talk about."

V rolled her onto her back. "That's their problem. Right now, I have a need to kiss you."

"What are you waiting for?" she asked seductively, wrapping her arms around his neck.

CHAPTER SIX

The stars were bright in the night sky as Claire bundled herself
in several blankets and sat in front of the firepit. She perched
in V's lap as they gazed at the loch. They rested in silence,
simply enjoying being in each other's company. No one from
the manor had contacted them, which meant that Pearl was
fine. Though Claire would have to return soon to nurse.

"V," she said on a gasp and pointed across the loch where
a large red stag stood drinking in the moonlight.

Suddenly, the animal lifted his head, turning to show his
impressive antlers.

"He's been coming for some time now," V said.

"He's beautiful."

V squeezed her. "That he is."

They continued watching the stag until he wandered back
into the shadows. V's heat kept the chill away. She was so
happy and content that she felt as if she could stay here
forever. Every time they came to his mountain, she understood

why he had chosen it. There was the beauty, of course, but that was everywhere on Dreagan. No, V's mountain and loch were special in ways she couldn't define. Maybe it was because he had chosen the location. Perhaps it was because he had spent so many lifetimes sleeping deep inside the mountain. Whatever it was, she felt him everywhere she looked.

"If we ever build our own place, I think this is a good spot," she said.

V kissed her temple. "I couldna agree more." He sighed softly. "As much as I want to stay, I think it's time we return."

"Can we come back?"

"As often as you want, love."

"But we're taking the blankets and stuff."

V chuckled. "Whatever you say."

He stood and carried her back into the yurt since she was barefoot. Claire wished she were more like V where the temperatures didn't affect her. They dressed, and he held out his hand for her. The minute she took it, they were back at Dreagan.

"That bracelet comes in handy," she said, nodding at Ulrik's piece of jewelry.

"I thought you might appreciate no' enduring the biting winds as I flew us to the mountain."

She smiled and gave him a quick kiss. "More than you could know."

They walked up the stairs to their chamber. Claire wore a smile as she entered, expecting to see Pearl. Instead, she found herself gazing into an empty room. She turned to her mate. "V?"

He said nothing as he led her out of the room and down the

hallway. Claire then found herself in what had once been Shaw's room. Except someone had moved all of her and V's things into it.

"I might have mentioned to Ulrik that we'd made a decision. He told me a few minutes ago that the changes had already been made," V said.

Claire moved into the room. The browns and earthy tones that V had chosen for himself before they met were still there. So were the table and chairs and the small sofa, as well as V's sword on the wall. The closet had all of their clothes and shoes exactly as they had been in the other room. Same with the bathroom. The only thing missing was Pearl's bassinet and the rocker.

When she turned to ask V about that, she found him standing by an open door in the wall that connected their chambers to another room. She walked up to him. He smiled before they entered together. There, she found the same wooden floors as throughout the house. The bassinet, rocker, and bags of baby items had been tucked against a wall in the room. But otherwise, the space was a blank slate.

"Whatever you want to do," V said from beside her. "Whatever furniture, whatever color. Your choice, my love."

"I shouldn't be surprised by any of this, but I am." She shook her head, grateful once more for the family she had found.

V pulled her against him. "Once you know what color you want the walls, let me know."

"I have a list."

"Now I'm the one who shouldna be surprised."

Claire laughed and shrugged. "I'm a planner. You know that."

V said, "Let's get comfortable, and then we can work on things."

"Are you sure? It's late."

He winked. "I'm sure."

"I love you so much." She rose on tiptoe and kissed him. "Where's Pearl?"

V sighed. "I'll find her."

Claire changed into a pair of comfy sweatpants, her favorite Ugg slippers that Rhi had gifted her, and a sweatshirt. Then she found the binder she had with all the things she had clipped and saved to decorate Pearl's room. She finished pulling her hair away from her face when V returned with Pearl. She took their daughter, who had begun to fuss. Claire brought Pearl into her new room to feed her.

V came in a short time later in a faded pair of jeans and a black *Def Leppard* shirt with her binder in hand. He opened it and flipped through the pages.

"Elder white for the paint color. I like it," he said and looked up at her. "I like it all."

She looked at the walls. "The elder white is the perfect mix of white and the faintest trace of taupe. So not a blinding white, but a good base to accent with other colors."

In a blink, the walls were elder white.

She took it in, nodded. "Yeah. I like it."

"I particularly love the 3-D butterflies. The rose gold color is perfect for Pearl," V said.

"My favorite crib is the white oval one."

They went through the binder for the next hour, picking

the things to decorate the room with. Claire loved how involved V was in everything.

"One more thing," he said.

Before she could ask, all the rugs from the yurt were suddenly there. Claire smiled, already thinking about which ones she wanted in Pearl's room and which she would rather put in theirs.

V stood with her as they put their sleeping daughter into her bassinet. V then took Claire's hand, and they walked into their room together. The door remained ajar so they could hear Pearl when and if she woke. They didn't need to because of the baby monitor, but they left it open anyway.

It was the wee hours of the morning before they finally climbed into bed. Claire lay on V's chest, his arm around her. So much happiness filled her heart, she thought it might burst. She squeezed V, who returned the gesture before kissing her forehead.

"We're verra lucky."

"So very much," she agreed.

He rubbed his hand up and down her back. "We have a daughter."

She smiled as she closed her eyes. "I know. She's pretty amazing."

"Because she takes after her mother."

"And her father." Claire shifted her head to kiss him.

She settled back into his arms and found herself starting to drift off to sleep. There was no better place than in V's embrace. Their love had made them strong. Malice might have been used to get her pregnant, but it was love and magic that had given them a daughter. And they had a family who would always have their backs.

"I love you," V whispered.

She smiled. "I love you more."

"I love you most."

SHARDS
of *Hope*

A Dark Kings Short Story

DONNA GRANT
NEW YORK TIMES BESTSELLING AUTHOR

CHAPTER ONE

Dreagan

Ulrik rolled over and reached for Eilish. His hand met the cool sheets of the bed. Instantly, his eyes were open. He looked from the empty spot beside him to the room at large, but his mate was nowhere to be seen. This was the fifth night in a row that he had reached for her and she wasn't there. Usually, she was in the room, but not this time.

He threw off the covers and rose from the bed, grabbing a pair of sweatpants that he had discarded over a chair. He shoved his legs inside them and was out the door. Once in the corridor, he peered first one way, then the other. The manor was quiet with light coming from the moon spilling through the windows and the soft glow of a lamp from beneath the bottom of a couple of doors.

Ulrik knew Eilish wouldn't disturb any of the other couples, but he was concerned enough to find her. He strode toward the stairs and looked over the banister. He caught a glimpse of her robe before it vanished out of sight. Ulrik launched himself over the rail and landed silently on the main floor.

He turned his head the direction Eilish headed and followed. Her silver robe billowed behind her as she walked through the moonlight as silent as a ghost. She paused outside the library and reached for the handle. Ulrik stilled, watching. Waiting. A red-orange glow of firelight seeped beneath the bottom of the doors. A feminine laugh sounded from within, followed by a deeper, masculine chuckle. Another Dragon King and his mate were inside. Eilish lowered her hand and continued walking. Ulrik followed her, his unease growing.

He started to call out to his mate when she diverted and headed into the conservatory. He was some twenty paces behind her when he slipped into the room. It was easy to spot her long, dark locks and the bright sheen of her silk robe among the greenery. As she meandered through the plants, her hand rose, fingers caressing each leaf and flower. The long, bell-shaped sleeves of the robe fell back to expose the winding tattoos on her arms, made of the same special red and blink ink that marked each King with their dragon tattoos. There were more of the winding tats on her legs. They were from a time when he had nearly lost her. She had been trapped… somewhere. They still didn't know where it had been, but he'd found her and brought her back, none the worse for wear other than the new tattoos.

They didn't bother her, or so she said. But Ulrik knew that she had received them for a reason. They might not know what that was yet, but he suspected they would eventually.

What bothered him the most was how her tats were the same color as a King's. Magic gave them their tattoos. Was that what had marked Eilish? Was that what kept her up?

Ulrik saw her profile when she turned to the side. Her beautiful face was pinched in worry lines. His heart clutched. What was wrong with his mate that she couldn't tell him? They shared everything.

Or they usually did.

Something bothered her enough to keep her from sleep. And from telling him. That would end tonight. Whatever it was, they would deal with it. Together. It's how they had defeated his uncle. It's how they approached everything.

Ulrik cut through one of the aisles of plants and started toward her. The tall, potted trees prevented him from keeping his eyes on her. When he emerged, he saw her glide through the hidden door that exited into Dreagan Mountain, a place he and the other Dragon Kings used before and after their patrols of the sixty thousand acres they called home in the Scottish Highlands.

He trailed Eilish into the mountain. The tunnel was lit by the magic of the Dragon Kings. They could see as well in the night as during the day, but the mates didn't have such an ability. Her steps were purposeful as she strode through the twisting shaft, passing openings that led to other tunnels and caverns they used for meetings, interrogations, and, not so long ago, even as a prison.

Eilish stopped once she the tunnel opened up to the cavern at the back of the mountain. She crossed her arms over her chest and stared out the massive opening that was vast enough for the largest of them—which included himself as King of

Silvers, and King of Dragon Kings, Constantine—to fit through when they were in their true form. The cavern itself was enormous, with a ceiling that soared high above them and allowed natural light to spill in and showcase the dragon carvings that graced the walls. Many that he, himself, had etched into the rock.

She walked to one and stood before it. He hung back, watching curiously as she lifted a finger and traced the carving. When she sighed loudly and rested her forehead against the stone, he'd seen enough.

Ulrik came up behind her and covered her hand with his. Her head lifted and swung to him. He looked into her green-gold eyes and saw pain. "I think it's time you told me what's going on."

"I don't know," she whispered.

At the strain he heard in her American accent tinged with Irish, he pulled her against him. She wound her arms about him and rested her cheek against his chest. Ulrik kissed the top of her head and tamped down the mounting unease.

"Whatever it is, lass, we'll deal with it. Just tell me." When she didn't immediately reply, he said, "Please. I doona like you hurting. Let me help."

"I'm not sure you can."

"I know I can no' unless you share what's keeping you from sleep. And our bed."

Eilish raised her head and met his gaze. "I fall asleep. That's not the problem."

"Then what is?"

"The dream."

He frowned. "Dream. One dream?"

"The same every night for the last five."

His stomach clenched in dread. "What is it?"

"A cave."

Ulrik paused, wondering if he heard her right. "A cave? This cave?"

She shook her head. "I don't think so."

"Come," he said and took her hand to lead her back to the manor. "We're going to get you some tea so you can start at the beginning and tell me everything."

She threaded her fingers with his. "I wasn't excluding you. Or I didn't mean to make it feel as though I was. I'm just..." She shrugged.

"I know, love," he said and lifted her hand to kiss it.

They didn't speak again until they were in the kitchen. Ulrik sat her at the table and heated the water in the electric kettle. He lifted two bags of loose-leaf tea, both of which had come from Zora, the realm where their dragons resided. The tea was crafted by Nia, a resident of Zora who fell in love with Shaw, the quietest of all the Kings.

"Lavender chamomile or matcha rose?" he asked.

She shrugged, not bothering to look at either. "You pick."

Eilish loved tea. She chose her blends based on her moods. The fact that she was uninterested spoke volumes. Knowing his mate as he did, he made a cup of each. He leaned against the counter as they brewed. Eilish stared out the window with a faraway look, her dark waves falling becomingly against the silver of her robe. Beneath was a short slip of a gown in a slightly darker silver.

Ulrik added honey to both cups and brought them to the table. He sat the lavender chamomile before Eilish.

"Thank you," she said and wrapped her hands around the cup. After she warmed them, she took a sip of the brew.

Ulrik folded his hands together atop the table and waited.

She licked her lips and played with the handle of the mug. "There isn't much to tell. It's a cave."

"Describe it for me. We dragons tend to love caves. If I doona know of it, one of the others might. One way or another, we'll find it."

She took another drink, then set it aside and reached for his cup. After two sips, she wrapped her hands around the matcha rose blend, claiming it for her own. Ulrik grinned at her swap, but it wasn't unusual.

"It's dark and cold," Eilish said, a small wrinkle marring her brow.

He frowned as she shivered, as if she stood in the cave at that very moment. "Is anything in there with you?"

"No. I'm alone. Something keeps bringing me to the cave, to that exact spot."

"Can you see anything around you?"

"Rocks," she stated, shooting him a flat look.

Ulrik rested his hand atop her arm. "Did you see an entrance?"

"There is light. It's faint and coming from the side. In the dream, I try to turn toward it, but I can't. I'm staring at a wall."

"What's on it?"

"Carvings."

A fission of awareness shot through him. "What kind?"

"There's no design to it. It's like a child was let loose in there. Etchings on top of others. No discernable pictures or writing. At least none that I can make out."

Ulrik sat back and dropped his hands into his lap. Shock reverberated through him. It couldn't be. Surely not. He looked away as his mind struggled to make sense of what Eilish had told him. It had been eons of time, but no matter how much time passed, he'd never forget that cave. But…how could she know it? He'd told no one what he'd done within its walls.

And he wanted it to stay that way.

"The wind." Her gaze slid to him. "I hear wind in the cave. It howls, as if I'm—"

"Verra high up."

Her lips parted in shock. She searched his eyes for a long, silent minute. "Do you know this cave?"

Unfortunately. "Aye."

"Where is it?"

"The Caucasus Mountains." He had to be wrong. Please let him be wrong, but even as he silently said the words, he knew he wasn't. Whether it was something to do with Eilish being a Druid, or the magic that welled up on Dreagan, she had been shown his cave.

She nodded firmly. "I need to see it in person."

Blood rushed in his ears as dread soured his stomach. He broke into a cold sweat.

Eilish rose. "Let's go now."

"I-I'll tell you where it is." He could barely get the words out.

Slowly, she sank back down and studied him. "Tell me?" she repeated softly. "Why not take me?"

"I swore I'd never return. I willna. I *can no'*."

Her face went slack, and she squeezed her eyes closed briefly. "Of course. It's where you were during your banishment."

He nodded, unable to speak.

"The dreams want to show me something. I need to go," she told him. "I understand if you can't. I wouldn't want to return to a place like that either. But I have to go. There's something there for me to see."

"There's nothing there." He knew that for a fact.

She squeezed his hand. "I have to do this. I can't explain why."

Ulrik was so lost in memories that barely felt her lips on his as she kissed him. He watched her walk from the kitchen. He wanted to call her back, or to follow, but he couldn't. Those horrible recollections had hold of him. He thought he had faced them and accepted the past, but he hadn't. Not fully.

There was no reason for Eilish to see that cave, to see him at his worst. When madness had taken him. She would see how crazed his mind had been, how utterly unhinged. She might even discern how many times he had attempted to take his own life, only to continue to live. He had cursed the fact he was a King unable to be killed except by another King. He had cursed Con and the other Kings. He had cursed everyone and everything, his hate turning him into something that he hadn't recognized.

That place was a reminder of everything he had lost. When he'd ventured from that cave the last time, he'd vowed never to return. In all the centuries since, he hadn't.

He'd come back from that time of his life he wished he

could erase. He had once more taken his place with the other Kings at Dreagan, and he had found his mate. He wasn't that same person.

Or was he?

Was that what kept him away? Because the cave would show who he truly was? If Eilish saw, would she still love him? She could leave him and find another, but dragons mated for life. He was bound to her, heart and soul, for the rest of his life.

Ulrik stood up so fast the chair toppled backward. He rushed from the kitchen and took the stairs three at a time after her. He burst into their room to find Eilish dressed and putting on the silver finger rings that allowed her to teleport.

"Doona go," he pleaded.

CHAPTER TWO

Eilish had witnessed her mate in many circumstances, but she'd never seen him gripped by such trepidation. His breathing was rapid, and his eyes held a wild look about them that frightened her.

But his request cut her to her very soul.

Despite the many times they had spoken of his past, Ulrik was still held by it. The only way he would ever truly be free was when he faced it, and she wouldn't force him. It would have to be on his own terms. She knew he'd get there eventually, but that wasn't his issue tonight. It was about her seeing his past.

A part of him that remained forever, waiting for someone to stumble across it. He didn't care if it was strangers. They would never know who had marked up the walls or what he had been through that brought him to such a place. No, his concern was *her* seeing it.

She walked to him and placed her hands on his chest. "I

love you. Heart and soul, sweetheart. There is nothing from your past that scares me. You've told me all of it."

"Telling is one thing. Seeing…is quite another."

"You think I'll look at you differently."

A muscle jumped in his jaw. "I know you will."

"Then you don't know me at all if you believe that."

He turned away, shaking his head. "You willna be able to help it."

"It's just some drawings." She didn't point out that she had seen some of them in her dream. That might make things considerably worse.

He halted with his back to her, his hands braced on the wall, as if that was all that held him up. "I might have… glossed over some things when I told of you of that time."

"Do you remember when we met? You were still banished from Dreagan. You and Con so at odds that you wanted to challenge him for the position of King of Kings."

"Aye. I recall all of that."

"You told me then that you recognized the darkness I carried." She walked to him but didn't touch him. "You saw that darkness because you carried it as well."

He turned his head slightly. "You might have had some, but it was nothing to what I possessed."

"That darkness was anger, love. Rage and exasperation. And frustration. It might have consumed you for a time, but you set that aside. You joined Con and the other Kings to defeat your uncle. That decision led you back into the fold with your brethren. That's why you were so lost and enraged. You need them. You need Dreagan."

Ulrik blew out a breath and dropped his arms. Then, slowly, he faced her.

She cupped his face and stared into gold eyes as a lock of black hair fell over his forehead. He was a Dragon King. Commanding, powerful, cunning. Drop dead gorgeous. And hers. He had helped her through rough times. Just as she was going to be there for him now.

"I see you. The man who was betrayed by a lover, whose friends loved him so much they sought revenge on his behalf."

"A dragon who began the war with the humans and ruined everything."

She shook her head seeing some of the panic fade from his eyes. "That war would've happened eventually. That isn't solely on you. And trust me, Con knew what he did when he and the other Kings searched for your lover. You know what else I see?"

His gaze searched hers. "What?"

"I see a man who was utterly lost once. His soul adrift in a world he didn't understand or want. A man who came back from the very brink and found a path that he could walk. Maybe that path was originally set on bringing down his best friend, but in the end, that road led the two to reunite and wipe the past away. That path led you to me. To this very moment."

His shoulders dropped as he pulled her against him. She held him tightly, pouring all of her love between them.

They remained like that for several moments. Then, Eilish said, "One day, you should face the cave and whatever hold it has over you. I think it'll be what fully heals you so you can release the past once and for all."

"Your right," he whispered. "I'll go with you."

She pulled back and shook her head. "That's not what I meant. You need to go on your own time. If it means that much that I don't go until then, then I won't. Not until you're ready." As much as her dreams were shouting at her to find the cave, she would ignore them for him. Because she loved him that much.

"You said you needed to see the cave," Ulrik replied.

Eilish shrugged. "It can wait."

"The dreams are trying to tell you something."

"Maybe I'm reading too much into them."

He gave her a stern look. "You're a Druid, love. You never read too much into anything. We'll go."

"Honey, no," she said, trying to hold him when he walked away.

He paused and looked at her. "You're right about everything you said. I need to face the past."

"Not tonight." Why hadn't she realized the cave still upset him? She should've seen it, should've recognized his hesitation. If only she would've kept her mouth shut about needing to go that night.

He grinned, his eyes filled with an abundance of love. "I'm verra lucky. Do you know why?"

"Why?" she asked suspiciously.

His smile widened. "Because I have a beautiful, intelligent Druid who stole my heart. We do this. Tonight."

She started to argue, but he slipped out of her grip and walked to the closet to change. Within moments, he was back. He paused beside the bedside table and put on the silver cuff bracelet given to him by a Dark Fae imbued with their magic which allowed him to teleport.

It was a running joke among the Dragon Kings that the only two non-Fae at Dreagan who had that ability were mated. She never parted with her finger rings, but Ulrik was known to lend his bracelet to Kings who had need of it.

His shoulders lifted on a breath as he faced her. His features were set in determined lines as he returned to her side with a coat for her. Once she had it on, he held out his hand, waiting for her. Eilish eyed it as she considered refusing to go, but she knew that look in her mate's eyes. Ulrik was going with or without her. There's nothing on this Earth or any other realm that would prevent her from being with him in case he might need her. She slipped her hand in his.

"Prepare yourself," he said as his fingers closed over hers.

In the next instant, they stood within a dark cave. The cold was the first thing that she acknowledged. The wind whistled against the cold stones, but her gaze was locked on Ulrik. His breathing was shallow, his hold on her hand tight.

"It's just a cave. It's just a place you spent some time," she told him. "It has no hold over you."

He squeezed his eyes shut as a shudder went through his body. "Being here brings it all back in horrifying detail."

"Let's go home. We'll do this another time."

"Nay," he stated firmly. "I need a minute, is all."

She kept her eyes on him, ready to return to Dreagan on a moment's notice. But, as she watched, the tension began to ease from his body little by little. Eventually, he lifted his head and opened his eyes. He whispered something and his magic created light to fill the area.

"It's just a place," he murmured, repeating her words. "It's just a cave."

Her eyes burned with tears of pride. She couldn't imagine the onslaught of emotions he experienced, but he stood his ground, once more proving why the magic of this world had chosen him as King of Silvers. His gaze began to move over the walls. He didn't push away the emotions, but greeted each one, accepting it. Revulsion, alarm, panic. He flinched a couple of times, but gradually, it became easier for him to look at everything. Only then did she chance a look herself.

Her heart missed a beat when her eyes locked on the wall nearest her, because it was exactly as she had seen it in her dreams. Scribbles and marks that looked as if they might have been creating something before another image was drawn over it. A part of her wanted to try to discern each layer, but Ulrik tugged her after him as he ventured deeper into the cave.

That's when the drawings became clearer, more concise. They were remarkably done. The skill alone was mindboggling. Most of what Ulrik carved were dragons. Different sizes and in different situations from flying to sleeping to battling. Some were as small as her hand and others taking up most of the wall. Among the dragons were carvings of deer and an eagle or two.

As beautiful as these were to behold, she didn't know why she'd dreamed of this place. Perhaps there was nothing there for her. Maybe the dreams had been to remind Ulrik that he should come so he could heal fully.

Ulrik released her hand when he squatted down to peer at a carving near the ground. She walked around him to continue her perusal. All thought vanished like smoke when she found herself staring at…herself.

Her heart skipped a beat. She'd never felt so

discombobulated before. Simultaneously like a rug had been snatched from beneath her as well as if a piece of a puzzle had snapped into place. Eilish reached out a shaking hand and touched the markings of a face that was so exact it was like looking in a mirror. "How is this possible?"

"I have no idea," Ulrik said from beside her. "I drew everything, but I doona remember this."

Eilish turned and looked at the opposite wall. There, among more dragons, was her face, again and again. Some smiling, some serious. Some in profile, some facing forward. But there was no doubt it was her.

This was what she was supposed to see. "What does this mean? Did you see someone who looked like me?"

"Nay. I hated humans. I didna go near them. And they never ventured here."

She swung her head to him. "Does that mean…"

He met her gaze, shock reflected in his gold depts. "I saw you. Thousands of years before we were to meet, I knew your face. Every beautiful contour. I captured her courage, your beauty, and your power as precisely as you are."

There was no refuting what she saw, but she could hardly wrap her head around it. She swallowed and looked at one of the carvings. There was only one explanation for this: they had been destined for each other all along.

"I need to see something," Ulrik said.

She didn't have time to respond before he teleported them again. The light was gone, leaving her bathed in inky darkness. Ulrik began to pull her after him. She went two steps before tripping.

"Wait," she bade.

He might be fine striding in the blackness, but she wasn't. Eilish called to her magic and readied a chant to create fire, but Ulrik beat her to it. Another small ball of light rose above them.

"Sorry," he said with twisted lips. "I'm just in a hurry."

"Where are we?"

"My ancestral home in the Andes Mountains."

Another place he hadn't been back to since the war with the humans. There was excitement in his eyes as he studied her, waiting for her approval. She nodded. "Lead the way."

They set off with the light keeping pace with them overhead. The tunnel was large enough that she suspected Ulrik had traversed it in his true form. They didn't walk long. He drew her into a tunnel that branched off to the right which led to a sizable cavern.

The light rose, setting the entire space aglow and showing that it was filled with carvings. More of Ulrik's work. She grinned when she spied dragons. There also jaguars, llamas, and a condor or two.

"This way," Ulrik said.

She forced her gaze away from the walls and followed him as he searched for something. She hungrily ate up every little nugget that she saw of his past as questions filled her mind. She had to bite her lip to keep them to herself until later.

Suddenly, he stopped and pointed to a place on the wall where she saw her face again.

"After the mortals arrived on the realm and we shifted for the first time, I came here and drew for hours," he told her, his gaze locked on her drawing. "Half the time I didna know what I carved into the stone. It was here," he said and tapped his head, "and I needed to get it out." He looked at her. "You were with me even then."

Eilish looked back at her face carved in the stone, the eyes locked with hers. "Then we were destined."

"Aye, love," he said as he wrapped an arm around her. "It took eons to find you, though."

"Pretty sure *I* found you."

"Nay, lass. *I* did the finding."

They shared a laugh as she slid her eyes to him. It was amazing—startling—to know that Fate or destiny or whatever was at work had known all along of their love. It proved that each person had to navigate tricky terrain before they could find their person, the one that was the other half of them. But once they were found, everything made sense.

Ulrik's fingers caressed her face. "If you hadna dreamed of the cave, I would've never returned, and I would've never known that you've always been with me. Even in my darkest days."

"That means you were always with me, too."

He grinned. "We have proof. I wonder if any of the other Kings do?"

"I'd like to keep this our secret. This is ours." She glanced at the carvings. "I'm not sure it was meant to be shared with others."

"Anything you want. It was your love that helped save me."

She grinned and slid her arms around his neck. "You were already on that road. You just didn't know it. I only gave you a little push."

"I knew from the first that you were my mate. This confirms it. If you had any doubts."

"I never any doubts about you, our love, or our future. Now, shut up and kiss me."

He chuckled. "Bossy, wench. I like it."

"I know," she whispered right before his lips claimed hers.

"EPIC.
HEARTBREAKING.
THRILLING."
– #1 NYT BESTSELLING AUTHOR
RACHEL VAN DYKEN

A Warrior for Christmas

A DARK WARRIORS SPECIAL HOLIDAY NOVELLA

NEW YORK TIMES BESTSELLING AUTHOR
DONNA GRANT

DEAR READER—

When I started the Dark Sword series, I knew it would be something special. It all began with a question: Why did the Romans never conquer Scotland? A simple enough query that many historians believe they could—and have—answer(ed). However, since Rome wrote the history books, I've always wondered what the *real* reason was.

My love of Scotland and the Medieval period is where the series began. I was a historical writer then, and only a historical writer—until my editor asked me to be a contemporary writer. So, my beloved Warriors and Druids went from Medieval to modern-day. Unfortunately, because of that, my publisher insisted on a series name change. I fought to keep it the same because I knew readers would be confused, but I ultimately lost that battle. So, the *Dark Sword* series became the *Dark Warriors*.

I loved writing in the *Dark Sword/Dark Warriors* series. I loved everything about it. The heroes, the heroines, and, yes, even the villains. It wasn't the first series I ended, but it was one of the most difficult ones. Sure, I still wrote in the world, but I had to say farewell to the Warriors and Druids.

Except, I couldn't. Not completely. That's why I have them pop up in the other connected series throughout the Dark World. And each time I do—or did—there was an overwhelmingly positive response from readers. Which, of course, meant I had to keep doing it. That's why I wrote this holiday story. For *you*, the reader, who has begged and pleaded for more Warriors and Druids.

Yet, when I ended the *DS/DW* series, I honestly believed it would be the hard-stop end to them. It was why the epilogue at the end of Malcolm's book, MIDNIGHT'S PROMISE, gave a glimpse into each couple's future. But…since I couldn't leave the Warriors and Druids alone, that epilogue won't match up to what's happening now in the overall Dark World. My best advice is to take that epilogue and imagine it far, far, *far* in the future.

For now, I leave you with a holiday visit to MacLeod Castle…

xoxox,

DG

LUCAN AND CARA

December

MacLeod Castle

The gray sky stared back at Lucan as he gazed at the steady snowfall through the window. Behind him, his wife Cara sat on the floor, surrounded by different-sized pots in an assortment of colors as she sank her hands into the soil.

He'd built the conservatory especially for her. It didn't matter what season it was, Cara was always with her beloved plants. If she wasn't tending to one, she was planting seeds and helping them grow with her Druid magic as she was doing now. However, Lucan had wanted to give her a place to do so out of the weather.

Lucan had surprised her with the conservatory over two hundred years ago. In his opinion, it had been the best Christmas present he had ever given her. He had yet to gift her anything that even came remotely close in the years since.

"You're brooding."

Cara's sweet voice pulled him out of his thoughts. He grunted. "I'm no'."

"You forget, love. I know you better than you know yourself. Tell me what thoughts have pulled you under."

Lucan turned to her. Her brunette locks were pulled into a loose bun atop her head with wisps of curls falling to frame her heart-shaped face that he never tired of looking at.

She was covered in dirt from her elbows to her fingertips as she knelt before a large pot and stirred the soil with her hands. She always said there was nothing better than feeling the dirt between her fingers, and he happened to agree. Which was why he often helped her. He watched her cover the seeds in the soil and then place her hands atop it before letting her magic flow from her palms into the dirt. Within moments, seeds sprouted and grew tall, forming a lush bush with red berries. Mistletoe was always hung throughout the castle during December and used for the solstice, and Cara made sure there was always plenty.

She sat back with a smile and dusted off her hands. "That should do for now." She climbed to her feet and faced him. Her mahogany eyes searched his face. "What is it?"

Lucan walked to her and wiped a smudge of dirt from her cheek. "It's nothing, I assure you."

"Lucan MacLeod," she stated. "We don't keep secrets, remember?"

"It's no' a secret, darlin'."

"It is if you don't tell me."

He flattened his lips and sighed, knowing she wouldn't

give up until he told her. "I doona know what to get you this year."

"Is that all?" she asked with a laugh and shook her head.

"Is that *all*?" he repeated, slightly offended that she didn't see what a conundrum it was.

She put her hands on his chest and grinned up at him. "You don't need to get me anything. You know that."

"I like to see you opening my gifts."

"But I don't need anything."

"That isna the point," he argued.

She stepped back and began cleaning up the dirt that'd spilled during her work. "We've had over four hundred Yules, my love."

"I know." That was why it was so difficult for him to find something to give her. His wife was simple in her desires—plants. He had gotten seeds from all over the world for her until there was no more to give. Maybe he should ask the Dragon Kings if they could bring some from Zora. The realm was similar to Earth but different enough that there might be new flora.

Cara straightened, dusted off her jeans, and caught his gaze. "I have all I need with you."

"I appreciate that, but—"

"But you're still going to get me something," she said with a shake of her head.

Lucan lifted the heavy pot and carried it off to the side to put with the other mistletoe plants. "It gives me pleasure." He watched her pause beside another plant and whisper to it. "You doona seem to have the same problem finding gifts for me."

She glanced at him over her shoulder and smiled slyly.

"What's your secret?" he pushed.

Cara faced him and shrugged. "If I find something that reminds me of you, then I get it."

"That's it?" It couldn't be that easy. She always gave him terrific gifts.

She laughed. "Ever since you presented me with the conservatory, you've been trying to outdo it. There's no need."

He disagreed. He remembered the look of utter joy on her face when he showed her the inside. She hadn't been able to stop touching the pots, bags of soil, and the seed packets waiting for her. They had locked themselves in the room for the rest of the day. Between rounds of sex, he'd helped her begin her indoor garden. Not a day went by that she wasn't in the conservatory.

"How many times have we mulled over the fact that so many things had to go right for us to meet?" she asked.

Lucan raked a hand through his black hair. "Too many to remember."

"And how many times have we considered everything we had to go through to triumph over Deirdre, Declan, and Jason?"

Just the mention of the Druids who had sought to control Warriors like him made Lucan's heart skip a beat. The primeval gods inside each Warrior had been called up from Hell to defeat Rome, but the Druids hadn't been able to return them. So, the gods had moved through the bloodline to the strongest in each clan. Lucan shared the god Apodatoo with his two brothers. Where they'd once thought it meant the end of everything, their immortality had opened up another world, ushered in by Cara's arrival to the castle that fateful day in

1603. After three hundred years in the crumbling ruins of his castle, there was suddenly someone else. And not just anyone. Cara. A beautiful temptress who had enticed him beyond reason. She had brought sunshine into his dreary life.

"Numerous," he answered.

Cara smiled gently, her dark eyes showering him with love. "You, Fallon, and Quinn survived the god within you when so many others succumbed."

"Because it was divided between us." To this day, Lucan wasn't sure if any of them would have been strong enough to take control of the god had it gone to only one of them.

Cara walked to him and took his hands, placing them on her waist before looping her arms around his neck. His sea green eyes held hers as she smoothed a strand of his black hair back from his face. She thought about the day they'd met. She had been picking mushrooms near the cliffs, and the land had given way beneath her. Lucan had caught her before she plunged to her death.

"I discovered that I was a Druid," she said. "You gave that to me."

He shook his head. "That wasna me, darlin'."

"I would never have found out had Deirdre not attacked. So, aye, I consider that a gift."

Lucan grinned at her. "You gave me my life back. Before you, I merely existed here, thinking about the days when our clan was strong and plentiful while living in the ruins of the castle, the clan gone. Because of us."

"You and your brothers not only prevailed over your god but also kept Deirdre at bay when she would've captured you for her army of Warriors."

"I wasna the only one to triumph. You, my beautiful wife, stood against Deirdre, too. The *drough* was formidable, but you didna back down."

"Because you were there. The love between us kept me going, even when all seemed lost."

She didn't like to think about the times they had nearly fallen to Deirdre. The Druid had been powerful and relentless. There had been instances she had been sure they would lose. But, somehow, they'd managed to come out on top until they ultimately defeated her.

"Word spread quickly," Cara continued. "Other Warriors who hadn't succumbed to the wills of their gods came to MacLeod Castle. You and your brothers took them in. You created your own army, one that intended to stand against Deirdre and any *drough* after her who sought to use the Warriors for their gain."

"We lost our clan—our blooded family. But in turn, we found another. No' just Warriors, but Druids of incredible strength and power."

"So, see, my Warrior? You've given me more than I ever thought possible."

He kissed her gently. "I appreciate what you're doing, but I still want to have something wrapped for our celebration."

The winter solstice was a day that everyone at the castle celebrated together. Each couple spent Christmas together separate from the group, but they gathered again for a big celebration on Boxing Day. It had been their tradition for more decades than Cara could remember.

She looked at her handsome husband. "I can go a year without something."

"All right. I'm game to do that. If you doona get *me* anything."

Her lips parted. "I…I can't do that. I already bought your gift."

"Then we're exchanging."

"There's no rule that says each of us has to give the other a gift."

Lucan leaned his head back and laughed. "That's pretty much the premise."

"It doesn't have to be."

He lifted her with a sexy smile she knew well. She wrapped her legs around his waist as he held her securely. Lucan kissed her softly before whispering, "When you stop giving me gifts, I'll stop giving them to you."

"That's not fair," she said between kisses. "I like finding things for you."

Lucan chuckled. "Then I suppose we'll both have to deal with it."

"Hmm," she murmured as the press of their lips lingered. She leaned back and looked at him. "There is an early gift you could give me."

He quirked a brow. "Oh? What might that be?" he teased.

She glanced at the open door. "Remember when you gave me this incredible room?"

His cock hardened against her.

"You do," she said with a sexy grin. "Get the doors?"

Lucan didn't have to be told twice. He released her and strode to the doors, shutting and then locking them. When he turned back, she had already pulled out the blankets and pillows they stashed there for just such an occasion.

She yanked off her clothes in record time and then released her hair and crooked a finger at him. Lucan ate up the space between them and yanked her against him.

"Och, woman. How you make me ache."

With heavy-lidded eyes, she yanked open his shirt. Buttons went flying in all directions. "Then let me ease you."

He was naked in seconds. Desire consumed her as he cupped her breasts and thumbed her hard nipples. He lowered her to the blankets and took her mouth in a searing kiss as her fingers wrapped around his length.

A storm roiled outside, and another kind raged within the conservatory—one they both sought, chasing the pleasure they knew awaited them.

MISTLETOE KISS COCKTAIL

INGREDIENTS:

For the rosemary simple syrup*:

- ½ cup water
- ½ cup granulated sugar
- 1 sprig rosemary

For a small batch:

- 6 oz vodka
- 1 oz freshly squeezed lemon juice
- 2 oz rosemary simple syrup
- Club soda
- Handful of fresh cranberries (whole frozen berries are fine)
- 2 sprigs of rosemary

For a large batch:

- 30 oz vodka (3 ¾ cups or approximately 1 liter)
- 5 oz freshly squeezed lemon juice
- 10 oz (1 ¼ cups) rosemary simple syrup (triple the recipe above)
- 1 liter club soda
- ½ bag of fresh cranberries (or whole frozen berries)
- 10 sprigs of rosemary

<u>INSTRUCTIONS:</u>

To make the rosemary simple syrup:

Combine the water and sugar in a small saucepan set over medium-high heat. Bring to a boil while stirring occasionally to dissolve the sugar. Allow the mixture to boil for 5 minutes and then remove from the heat and drop in the sprig of rosemary. Allow the rosemary to steep for about 15 minutes and then discard the sprig. Pour the simple syrup into a glass jar or bottle, cool to room temperature, cover, and refrigerate.

To make a small batch:

Pour vodka, lemon juice, and simple syrup into a drink shaker filled with ice. Cover and shake well to blend. Divide drink mix between 2 rocks glasses filled with ice, straining the ice from the shaker as you pour. You'll only want to fill the glasses ¾-full. Top with club soda and a few cranberries for garnish. Add a sprig of rosemary to use as a stirrer.

To make a large batch:

Pour vodka, lemon juice, and simple syrup into a pitcher filled with ice and stir well to combine.

When ready to serve, pour the drink mix into an ice-filled rocks glass to ¾-full. Top each drink with club soda and a few cranberries for garnish. Add a sprig of rosemary to each drink as they are served to use as a stirrer.

If you make the large batch before your guests arrive, be sure to keep the pitcher in the fridge to ensure the drinks are icy-cold when they arrive.

NOTES:

*The rosemary simple syrup recipe above will make more than you need for a small batch, but the leftovers store well in an airtight container, like a mason jar, in the fridge for up to 2 weeks.

PARTY TIME TIPS:

If you plan to serve this drink at a party, here are a few tips for prep:

1. Print out instructions so your guests know how to assemble the drinks and post at your drink station.
2. Ready an ice bucket filled with ice as well as drink glasses so guests can help themselves to drinks from the pitcher.
3. Have a small bowl of cranberries ready to go.
4. Stand the rosemary sprigs up in a small glass.

FALLON AND LARENA

Larena sang along to *A Holly Jolly Christmas* by Burl Ives, blaring from the speakers in the great hall as she made her way to Fallon's office. It had once been a solar, but they had long ago converted it into an office during one of their many castle remodels.

She bit into a gingerbread cookie as she leaned against the doorway and watched her husband and fellow Warrior, Fallon. As the eldest of the MacLeod brothers, he took his duties seriously. Sometimes, too seriously. He was also the leader of the Warriors and Druids who called the castle home. Which meant he felt the weight of responsibility.

Not that she let him carry it alone. They shared many of the obligations, but being a laird and all that entailed had been ingrained in Fallon from a young age. Those who lived at the castle were a different kind of clan than those who had once resided here, but Fallon was still very much a laird.

His dark brown hair was on the long side and disheveled

from him running his fingers through it. His brow was furrowed, and his lips were drawn tight. He wore a hunter green Henley shirt that made his dark green eyes pop even more. A shadow of a beard covered his chiseled jaw, and his gold torc gleamed just beneath his shirt. She caught sight of the boar heads on each end.

"If you're going to stare, the least you could do is share the cookie," Fallon said without looking up from the paper he studied.

Larena grinned as she pushed away from the doorway and walked to the desk. "You know I don't share cookies. However, I brought one for you."

He lowered the paper and looked up at her with a smile. Even after so many centuries together, he could still make her heart skip a beat as it had from the first moment she'd seen him. She handed him one of the cookies as she sat on the edge of the large, wooden desk.

Fallon leaned back in the chair and bit off the head of the gingerbread man. "Hmm. Just what I needed."

"You can thank Reaghan. I didn't think it was possible for her to better her recipe, but somehow, she did."

"Or she used her magic."

They shared a smile.

Larena finished her cookie and glanced at the papers Fallon had been poring over. She noted Vaughn's name. The Dragon King was a solicitor for Dreagan, but he also did work for the Warriors.

"It's the final bit of paperwork to secure the land that's rightfully ours once and for all," Fallon said.

She looked into his dark green eyes. "It was the right way

to go. It would've been too much to prove you are who you are since everyone believed the MacLeod clan had been wiped out."

"Vaughn was correct, but it doesna make things any easier. This land was my birthright. I should be happy that it's ours now. And I am."

"But?" she pressed.

He sighed as he shrugged a shoulder. "People like us doona get peace for long, sweetheart."

"Ah. You're referring to the Skye Druids." She leaned back on her hands and looked around at the framed photos of MacLeod Castle through the four hundred years they had lived here. "You're right. People like us don't get normal lives. We were chosen for these roles. We've succeeded multiple times in the past, and we will continue to do so."

Fallon studied her for a long moment. "What did I ever do to deserve you?"

"You're just lucky, is all," she said with a grin.

"Aye," he replied seriously.

She frowned as she sat up. "You're worried."

"I'm always worried. Everything we have here is fragile. We lived apart from the rest of the world for hundreds of years. The magic Isla used to hide the castle kept the Druids from aging, as long as they stayed in it. Thanks to our friendship with the Dragon Kings, they can now leave the castle without fear of aging. We were the only ones who didna have to worry about that since you're a Warrior."

Larena grimaced as she recalled those difficult years when none of the Druids had left the castle grounds. "But that's behind us now. You can't think about the problems that will come next because there will always be something."

"It's my duty to try and foresee any issues and be prepared."

"You're a Warrior, handsome," she said as she slipped from the desk and straddled his lap. "Not a god. You can only do so much. Besides, you do too much now."

"*We* do," he corrected.

She winked at him. "We can never prepare for everything, but we're strong. We have friends who have come to our aid, and we have gone to theirs. That's how we keep prevailing against those trying to shift the balance in their favor. We're not in this alone."

"Did anyone ever tell you how wise you are?" he asked with a grin.

Larena shot him a flirty smile. "There is this one guy. Handsome as sin, he is."

"Is that right?" Fallon asked with narrowed eyes.

She nodded. "Oh, yes. He's an amazing lover, too."

"I doona think I like this man."

"I could introduce you. Maybe you could learn a thing or two from him."

"Minx," he said as he yanked her against him and kissed her.

Larena sighed into the kiss, sliding her fingers into the cool strands of his dark hair. When Fallon ended the kiss, she jumped up and tugged on his hand. "You need a break."

"I still have work to do."

"It'll be there later. For now, you're mine."

Fallon followed behind his wife, feeling the dregs of the day falling away. Larena somehow always knew what he needed. She had her straight, golden blond hair in a loose braid today, and her smoky blue eyes seemed to grin at him as she looked over her shoulder.

She might be the only female Warrior, but Larena was so much more to him. Lover, friend, confidante, and partner. There wasn't anything about their lives they didn't share. She understood him as few could. She didn't demand that he change. Instead, she stood beside him and helped him shoulder whatever he carried.

He knew exactly how it would feel without her. Because he had lost her for a short time. She had been shot by those fighting the Warriors, and not by just any bullets. The X90 bullets were special. They contained wyrran blood—animals created by Deirdre to fight for her. Only the Druids, with their healing power, had been able to bring Larena back from the brink of death.

But when he'd thought she was lost to him, Fallon had discovered what his life would be like without her. The stark emptiness was even more damning than what he had experienced after the god had been released and inhabited him and his brothers. He'd only *thought* he knew pain and loneliness. He hadn't really known, not until he believed Larena was lost to him.

Yet she had been brought back by the Druids. And he was grateful for every day he had with her. Warriors were virtually immortal, but that didn't mean they couldn't be killed. They weren't invincible. It was why he worried constantly about new enemies that may arise. Because his wife was right—they were the kind of people who fought against evil attempting to tip the balance to their side.

He let those thoughts drift away as Larena pulled him outside. The snow fell steadily and soon stuck to her hair and eyelashes as she released his hand and twirled around, laughing. Somehow, despite everything she had endured, Larena found a way to live each moment, whatever it might be, fully.

She reminded Fallon to embrace life and that not everything was doom and gloom. Because he knew he could sink deep into such thoughts. Whenever he did, she was always there to bring him into the light and shower him with love. He was the man he was now because of her.

He turned to look back at the castle. Just then, a snowball hit him square in the face. He blew the snow away and looked at Larena, who stood laughing. He wiped the rest of the snow from him. "Oh, you'll pay for that."

"Only if you catch me," she said as she turned and took off.

He raced after her, their gods giving them enhanced senses and the ability to run much faster than a human. She ran through the snow, zigzagging left and right to keep him guessing. But he was gaining on her.

As he ran, he scooped up handfuls of snow and packed a ball tightly. When it was big enough, he tossed it at her. It landed on her shoulder, showering her with snow. Her laughter trailed after her as she continued to run. Fallon's smile was huge as he pumped his legs faster, gaining ground. Just as he was about to catch her, she veered to the left. He skidded as he turned and hurried after her once more.

"I thought you were faster than that," she taunted over her shoulder.

Fallon felt the god within him thrill when he called for more speed. Then, he had her. He looped an arm around her waist and yanked her against him as he turned and dropped them into a thick pile of snow, rolling until he was on top of her.

"I always catch you," he told her, breathing heavily.

In a blink, she had him on his back, her legs straddling him. "Maybe I *let* you catch me."

"Oh, I know you better than that." He pulled her down for a kiss. "Thank you."

"For what?"

He caressed her face. "For knowing when I need a break. For giving me reasons to smile and laugh. And love."

"My pleasure."

"You're getting wet."

"So are you. I guess that means we should get out of these clothes," she said with a knowing look.

Fallon grabbed her hips and rocked her against his erection. "I do like the way you think."

"The bed? Or the bath?"

"Why no' both?"

They jumped up together and strolled, hand in hand, toward the side of the castle. Then, they used their powers and jumped to the battlement wall so they could climb the cold stones to the window of their room.

They came together in a flurry of kisses and hands, each

trying to get the other's clothes off first. Larena laughed breathlessly as she gazed up at him. "I love you."

"And I love you," he said as he backed her toward the bathroom that housed their large tub, big enough for two.

Larena started the water and returned for another kiss. One item at a time, they divested each other of their remaining clothing before they got into the tub of steaming water.

GINGERBREAD

COOK TIME:

Prep: 1 hour 45 min

Cook: 8 min

Total: 1 hour 53 min

SERVING SIZE:

3 – 4 dozen

INGREDIENTS:

Gingerbread:

- ¾ cup unsalted butter
- ¾ cup brown sugar, packed
- ¾ cup molasses or syrup
- 1 teaspoon salt
- 2 teaspoons cinnamon
- 2 teaspoons ground ginger

- ¼ teaspoon allspice
- 1 egg
- 1 teaspoon baking powder
- ½ teaspoon baking soda
- 3 ½ cups all-purpose flour

Frosting:

- 2 cups powdered sugar
- 1 teaspoon vanilla
- 4 tablespoons milk

INSTRUCTIONS:

1. In a medium saucepan, melt butter over medium-low heat.
2. Add brown sugar, molasses/syrup, salt, cinnamon, ground ginger, and allspice. Stir mixture together until well incorporated. Remove from heat.
3. Transfer mixture to a medium to large mixing bowl and add the egg and beat it in with the mixture.
4. In a separate bowl, add baking powder, soda, and flour and whisk together.
5. Add flour to the molasses mixture and stir together with a wooden spoon.
6. Divide dough into two equal halves. Over a sheet of plastic wrap, shape dough into a thick large rectangle and wrap each tightly. Refrigerate for at least one hour.

7. Preheat oven to 350°F. Line cookie sheets with parchment paper and set aside.

8. On a floured surface, roll dough into ¼-inch-thick rectangle with a floured rolling pin.*

9. Cut out shapes with gingerbread man cookie cutter or cookie cutter of choice. Place at least an inch apart on cookie sheets.

10. Bake for 8-9 minutes or until edges are browned. Let cool on cookie sheets for a few minutes and then transfer to cooling racks.

11. Once completely cooled, frost cookies or sprinkle with powdered sugar.

12. Store in airtight containers at room temperature or in freezer.

<u>NOTES:</u>

If flour seems sticky upon taking it out of the refrigerator, continue to sprinkle flour over dough and work it in with your hands until the consistency is improved and you are able to roll it out easier.

QUINN AND MARCAIL

Quinn didn't need to search the castle long to find Marcail. His wife was in one of the spare bedchambers upstairs, sitting on the floor, a thick pillow beneath her bum. An assortment of wrapping paper, colored ribbon, scissors, tape, and gift tags were all within easy reach. He grinned as he watched her tie an intricate bow. After she'd lifted the box and looked at it from all angles, she set it aside. Then she shot him a grin over her shoulder.

"Come to help?" she asked.

He chuckled as he carefully stepped over the rolls of wrapping paper. "I know better."

It was her turn to laugh. "That's right. This is my thing."

It wasn't that Marcail didn't love decorating for the holidays, but she had a passion for wrapping. Stacks of different-sized and shaped boxes grouped by color rested in locations around the empty chamber. She spent hours at a time in the chamber, working on each box, wrapping it to perfection before tying it off with incredible bows.

Most of the couples handed the wrapping duties over to Marcail. While Tara and Aisley liked to do their own, all the men brought their gifts to his wife to wrap. Everyone, that was, except for him. He'd learned his lesson after getting Marcail to wrap her own gifts one year. He hadn't made that mistake again. Instead, he set about learning how to wrap as beautifully as she did.

Well, it wasn't as nice, but it was close.

He'd do anything to keep her happy and learning how to wrap was nothing. Now, he leaned a shoulder against the wall and studied the sets of gifts. Each year, he tried to determine which color paper belonged to which couple. Marcail didn't just love wrapping, she adored shopping for the paper, too. The girls usually spent an entire day finding just the right paper and ribbon to match their decorations.

"You'll never guess this year," she said with a grin.

Quinn had never gotten them all right. It wasn't easy since each couple switched colors every year. Never in his wildest dreams would he have thought to have two rooms in the castle devoted to nothing but storage for Christmas. There were twenty trees—because the castle always had more than one, and there were extras for anyone who wanted to use one. Then there were the boxes of ornaments and decorations—organized by color, of course.

And who did all of that? His beautiful wife.

It was up to each couple to decide on the tree and color before telling Marcail so she could make sure everyone had what they needed to decorate. Every year, the girls came back from one of their many shopping trips with more decorations, and, of course, tote boxes to organize everything.

Marcail looked up from cutting paper. "What are you grinning about?"

"I'm wondering how long it'll be before the holiday decorations need a third room."

Her smile widened. "Sooner than you might think."

"All right," he said and rubbed his hands together. "Let's get to this."

His eyes scanned the presents. They weren't huge piles. Instead, each couple only had a handful of gifts each. He counted fourteen groups, which meant Marcail had wrapped some for everyone. By the stacks of boxes beside her, she still had a few to go. He didn't know how she kept up with whose was whose, but she always did—all without looking inside. He wouldn't be able to keep from peeking. Which was one reason he wasn't allowed in the room with her for long. He only had so much fortitude before he caved and reached for an unwrapped box.

"Do I need to kick you out now?" Marcail asked without looking at him. "You're eyeing the unwrapped boxes already."

Ah, his beautiful wife knew him too well. He grinned at her. "I'm in complete control."

"Right." She laughed.

He couldn't even argue with her because she was right. And she knew it. Then again, Marcail was usually always right. She shot him a side-eye, which made him return his attention to the wrapped bundles.

First up, a set with each package wrapped in a different green plaid. She'd used white, black, and different shades of green ribbon. The gift tags were a green so dark they almost looked black.

Then came the blue. The paper was solid, matte navy with gold velvet ribbons and matching gold gift tags.

There was a rustic white and linen-colored set. The wrapping was either brown kraft paper or white with natural designs, along with linen and white-colored ribbons to match. The tags were natural-colored.

Next was the soft gray and pale pink collection. There was narrow gray-and-white-striped paper, all white, white with gray ornaments, pink, and pink with gold snowflakes. Marcail varied the ribbon combination on the packages and added pink name tags.

Finally, he came to the red—historically his favorite. She'd mixed the bold red and black buffalo check with cream paper that had a pearlescent finish. The plaid had been paired with cream velvet, while she'd used black ribbon edged with red glitter with the cream. The gift tags were black with red lettering.

That brought him to the burgundy and gold. It was a muted burgundy, the paper looking as if it had been scraped. Marcail used gold or burgundy velvet ribbon edged with metallic gold. The name tags were gold.

His gaze landed on the packages wrapped in a deep, metallic teal. Each had a dried orange slice tied with a copper-colored ribbon. Tucked against the orange were sticks of cinnamon and sprigs of rosemary. The gift tags were copper.

Then came the metallics—lustrous bronze, silver, gold, and copper paper. Matching ribbons of different widths—and name cards—were alternated to create a stunning vision.

When he saw the next packages, he decided to change his favorite for the year. Some boxes were wrapped in matte black paper with red ribbon, while others had a small-check black and red plaid with either black or red ribbon. The gift tags were a metallic red.

Next up was the white and silver group. From metallic silver to white paper and several combinations of both, they drew the eye. White and silver ribbons and matching gift tags completed the assortment.

His gaze shifted to the next pile of gifts in rose gold paper with different holiday designs. All were finished with elaborate gold, white, and rose gold ribbons and white gift tags.

The next group consisted of shimmery lavender and matte white paper. The presents were finished with either glittering lavender ribbon or white tulle and had lavender gift tags.

A unique green and gold combination was next. The greens ranged from sage to hunter, and every paper had a design in gold. The boxes were completed with velvet, shimmery, or glittery gold ribbon and green gift tags.

Last was an icy blue, silver, and white paper set. The ribbons were a metallic silver, glittery pale blue, and navy with icy blue tags.

"Well?" Marcail said as she got to her feet and faced him.

Quinn pointed to the matte black and red set. "That's ours."

"Oh?" she asked, giving nothing away.

He nodded, feeling surer by the second. "My skin changes to black when I release the god inside me, and you know how I love red."

"I've not used black before. Why would I now?"

His grin widened. "Because I know you."

Marcail couldn't hold back her smile. "It seems you do."

"I like the combination. Great choice."

She beamed because she loved when he got excited about such things. "Care to try the rest?"

"The royal blue and gold are for Fallon and Larena."

"Two in a row. Good start."

His sly smile told her he planned to get it all this year. "The metallics are for Lucan and Cara."

Her brows shot up on her forehead. "Three in a row."

"The rose gold is for Ramsey and Tara."

"Keep going," she urged.

Quinn pumped his fist in the air before looking over the remaining ten groups. "The green plaid, I think that's for…" he said, dragging out the *r*, "hm. Maybe…Camdyn and—no, no' Camdyn. I say Ian and Danielle."

"You nearly bungled that one. Yes, it's for Ian and Dani."

"My best is nine in a row. I'm going to beat it this year," he told her.

Marcail smiled. It was a silly game they played, but it was theirs, and she cherished every second.

"The rustic white and brown is for Galen and Reaghan. The gray, pink, and white is for Laura and Charon, and the red and black plaid is for Broc and Sonya."

"Correct on all three."

"One more to tie my record," Quinn said to himself as he

rubbed his hands together. He cleared his throat and said, "The burgundy and gold belongs to Phelan and Aisley."

"Well done," Marcail complimented.

He winked at her. "The teal is…" He paused, tapping his fingers on his chin. "Give me a second."

Marcail watched him, silently saying the names in her head and hoping he got them right.

His pale green gaze slid to her. A lock of his light brown hair fell into his eyes, but he didn't seem to notice. "The teal is for Isla and Hayden."

She didn't answer right away, because what was the point of the game if she couldn't have any fun?

"You're killing me, lass. Did I get it right?"

Marcail finally caved and nodded.

"Yes!" he bellowed and pumped both fists. "Four more to go."

"If you get them all this year, it will make it harder for next year."

He shot her a perturbed look. "Doona distract me, woman."

That only made her smile. As he considered the last four, her mind turned to their son, Aiden, and his wife, Britt. Thankfully, Quinn didn't leave her to her thoughts for long.

"The white and silver is for Ar—I mean Logan and Gwynn." His gaze searched hers. "Am I correct? Tell me I'm right."

"You are."

Quinn's smile was blinding. "That means the lavender is for Camdyn and Saffron."

"It is."

"Two to go," he murmured, concentrating on the last two sets.

"The ice blue is Malcolm and Evie's, and the sage green is for Arran and Ronnie."

She blinked, shocked that he had finally gotten them all right after all these years. "I can't believe it."

Quinn walked to her and wrapped his arms around her, lifting her so he could turn her in a circle. "I knew I'd get it one day." He kissed her and then gently set her on her feet. "Now, tell me what's wrong."

She was so taken aback by the subject change that it took her a moment to realize what he'd said. "What?"

"I spoke with Sonya downstairs. She said you've been distracted. It's about Aiden, is it no'?"

Marcail should've known she couldn't hide it from him. "Aye. I hate that they won't be here for the solstice, Christmas, or Boxing Day. We've always had at least one winter holiday with them."

"Ah, love," he said and brought her against his chest. "It's only one year. We see them all the time."

"But it's the holidays," she argued.

Quinn kissed her on top of her head. "They'll be here for New Year's. They deserve to have time to themselves."

"I agree. Just not when families are supposed to be together."

He rubbed his hands up and down her back. "We've always done our best to give them space. Our son's upbringing was different because he wasna a Warrior. He's a Druid, but we can no' keep him here."

"I know." He wasn't saying anything that Marcail hadn't

told herself a hundred times. But she missed her son and daughter-in-law. It didn't seem right that they weren't here.

Quinn leaned away to look at her. "Do you remember what it was like for you, no' being able to leave the castle lands?"

"Aye. I hated it."

"Which is why we're no' going to do the same to Aiden and Britt." He pulled her against him once more. "Doona think I'm no' missing them because I am. I'm just trying hard no' to let it show."

That made her smile. "I know you are. Thank you."

"I did warn them that they would have to make it up to us when they got back."

Marcail was the one to lean back this time. "A party?" she asked excitedly.

"Ah, my love. The biggest one you want to have."

"Can we invite the Dragon Kings? What about Rhona and Balladyn? Oh, and the rest of the Reapers?"

He laughed and smiled as he rubbed his nose against hers. "Anyone you want."

"I have so much planning to do," she said as she glanced at the rest of the presents she had to wrap.

Quinn held her when she tried to move away. "Nay, lass. No' quite yet," he said in that husky voice she knew so well.

Her stomach quivered in excitement as she met his lips for a kiss.

NON-ALCOHOLIC MULLED WINE

COOK TIME:

Prep: 5 min
Cook: 30 min
Total: 35 min

SERVING:

8 cups

EQUIPMENT:

Fine mesh sieve
Ladle
Citrus juicer

INGREDIENTS:

- 2 large oranges, divided
- 64 oz cran-grape juice

- 6 whole cinnamon sticks
- 4 whole star anise
- 8 whole cloves

INSTRUCTIONS:

1. Slice one orange into thin wheels and juice the second orange.
2. Place orange slices, juice, cinnamon sticks, cloves, and star anise in a large saucepan or Dutch oven. Bring just to a boil, reduce heat and simmer for at least 20 – 30 minutes (see notes below), stirring occasionally.
3. Strain juice through mesh sieve. Return juice to pan and stir in reserved orange juice. Serve warm and garnish with additional orange slices and whole spices, if desired.

NOTES:

- No cran-grape juice? Use half a bottle of grape juice and half a bottle of cranberry juice instead. Or just grape juice.
- Make this recipe up to 3 days ahead of time. It can be frozen for up to 2 months.
- The 30-minute simmer time is a starting point. The longer the juice simmers with the spices, the more flavorful the drink will be.
- Can also be made in a slow cooker. Mull ingredients in slow cooker for at least two hours.

HAYDEN AND ISLA

Isla finished knitting the blanket and held it up to look it over. She was happy with the outcome. Most especially that she'd decided on an ombre pattern. The off-white to cream to beige to brown was really eye-catching. But her favorite thing about it was the cabled wave pattern.

She set aside the blanket and put away the yarn and her needles. Isla glanced out the window of her home perched near the cliffs and sighed at the beauty.

"It never gets old, does it?" Hayden said as he walked up behind her.

She didn't need to ask to know that he referred to the spectacular view of the sea. "Never."

"The snowfall is going to get worse as the day goes on. Should make for a beautiful solstice tomorrow."

Isla leaned back against her husband as he wrapped his arms around her. This was her favorite time of year. It didn't matter the kind of weather they had, it was always magical. "It's stunning, but I think this year will be special."

"Oh?" he asked, his chest rumbling with his deep voice. "Why is that?"

"Just a feeling."

There was a slight pause, then he asked, "Have the Ancients spoken to you?"

"No." Unfortunately, she hadn't heard the Ancients since they'd been cut off the last time she and the other Druids had heard them. She would've thought she'd dreamed the entire thing if other Druids hadn't heard them, too. "I know they're picky about who they speak to and when, but this is concerning."

"They're the Ancients. I doona think you need to worry."

Isla hoped that he was right. She turned in his arms and gazed into his black eyes. He had his blond hair pulled back in a queue at the base of his neck, the top still damp from being out in the snow. "What's going on at the castle?"

"The usual," he said with a smile. "Utter chaos. I saw Lucan shut the door to the conservatory, which means that nobody will see him and Cara for several hours."

Isla laughed. "They do love that room."

"Larena managed to get Fallon out of his office. I heard Quinn shout for joy, so I think he might have guessed everyone's colors this year."

"It's taken him long enough," she replied with a chuckle.

"There are fourteen couples."

She bit her lip. "But sixteen Warriors."

There was a pause before he said, "Dale?"

Isla heard the reproach in his voice and hid her wince. "He is one of you."

"He worked with Jason. Against us. That can no' easily be forgotten."

"No one is saying it has to be. But in the end, Dale prevailed. He got control of his god. He made a life for himself. He and Rennie."

"She bound his god."

"But he is still one of us. If we needed him, his god could be unbound."

Hayden sighed, his wide lips flattening into a firm line. "How long have you been planning to bring up Dale?"

"A wee bit."

"Why did you no' tell me?"

She gave him a pointed look. "Do you hear the way you're talking? That's why."

Hayden released her and stepped back before running a hand down his face.

"It's been years since everything happened with our enemies. We've made a life. Dale was left alone, but he found his way," Isla pressed.

"I admit to being surprised by that. You're no' the only one who's kept up with him. We thought we'd have to hunt him down and—"

"And kill him," Isla finished grimly. She twisted her lips. "It could've gone that route. He could've succumbed to his god and lost complete control, but he didn't."

Hayden grunted. "I'm thankful for that. I didna relish the idea of taking his life. But I would've done it if it meant saving others."

"I know. I would have, too." She went to him and took his hands in hers. "Isn't it time to let go of the past? Move forward? Dale and Rennie have never come to us or asked for anything. I'm not saying we should give them a room in the castle, but I'd like to invite them over for the solstice. Maybe they can come to dinner on Boxing Day next year if it goes well."

Hayden regarded her with his black eyes. "You know they may refuse."

"As is their right. But we need to reach out to them. You remember what it was like when you were alone, don't you? Before you found other Warriors?"

"It was bloody hell," he murmured.

She nodded. "It was."

"Shite. Now, I feel bad for no' thinking of this sooner."

Hope sprang up in her heart. "Does that mean you'll invite him?"

"It means I'll talk to the others about it. Fallon, Lucan, and Quinn keep saying the castle is our home, but it's theirs, first and foremost. I wouldna invite someone they didna want there. Same with the other Warriors."

"I understand."

She ran her hands over his muscular chest as she rose on tiptoe to kiss him. "Thank you."

"Doona thank me yet. Nothing may come of this."

"You listened to me, though."

"Och," he said with a frown. "I always listen. I may no' like what you say, but I listen."

She grinned and pulled his head down for another kiss.

Hayden held Isla's petite form tightly against him. Her straight, black hair hung down her back, brushing against the backs of his hands. When he straightened and looked into her ice blue eyes, he fought the urge to shield her from anything and everything bad in the world—though his wife needed no one to protect her. She was one of the most powerful Druids on Earth and could take care of herself.

But he was a protector. So, that's what he did. Isla had a good heart, and he didn't want her getting hurt. While he understood her reasoning about Dale, he was hesitant simply because he didn't want Dale to refuse them—which was a real possibility. The Warriors at the castle had turned their backs on Dale. They had thought him dead at first, but when they'd learned that he wasn't, they had been prepared to end his life if need be. They had fought too long and hard to have someone come after them again.

Hayden was soaked in the blood of his enemies, and nothing ever washed that away. The only thing that even came close was Isla's love. She had given it unconditionally from the start, even when he fought against his desire for her—fool that he was. But love had conquered his anger and hate.

Deirdre, one of their former enemies, had controlled Isla. It was likely why she sought to include Dale now. She knew what it was like to be on the wrong side of things. For many years, Hayden had woken up in a cold sweat when he thought about what could've happened to Isla had any other Warrior but him found her. They would've killed her.

Hayden had meant to take her life, but the way she'd

looked at him had stopped him. That same look told him how much inviting Dale and Rennie to the castle meant to her now. Despite the centuries of terror and pain that Deirdre had inflicted upon Isla, forcing her to do unspeakable things, Isla had found her way.

Just as Dale had.

Hayden smoothed a lock of Isla's midnight hair from her face. "You're something verra special."

"Because I'm yours," she replied.

"And I'm yours."

Isla smiled at him, giving him a look so filled with love that his heart skipped a beat. Suddenly, he was irritated that everyone had agreed to spend an extra night at the castle. He would prefer to carry his wife into their room and have his way with her for the rest of the day and into the night. But they could disappear to their chambers once they finished with dinner later. "Shall we go to the castle now?"

"Let me box up the blanket first."

"Is that your present this year?"

She beamed. "It is. It came out better than I'd hoped. I had no idea I'd love knitting so much. I'm thinking of making you a sweater next."

"I like the sound of that." He watched her lift the blanket and fold it neatly before putting it in a box and placing the lid on top.

For many years, everyone at the castle had bought gifts for each other and exchanged them during Boxing Day dinner. Several decades ago, they'd changed things up, and had everyone draw a name. The only caveat was that the gift had to be handmade by the person giving it.

Which made for some really fun—and sometimes funny—
and interesting gifts.

"You drew Camdyn's name, aye?"

"I did. Have you made your present for Broc yet?"

Hayden thought about the dagger he'd forged the day
before. "I need to finish the hilt."

"Check the boxes I have in the spare closet. I should have
one that will fit. And don't forget to use the tissue paper this
time. Pad it so the dagger doesn't move around."

He bit back his grin. "I'll be sure to do that."

She straightened and shot him a flat look. "You've seen the
stacks of tissue paper I have. There's plenty. Stuff it. Tight."

"I will," he replied firmly. "Trust me. I learned my lesson
last year."

Isla put on her boots and then her coat. Hayden grabbed
the box and met her at the door. They made their way to the
car. Normally, they walked to the castle. It was a bit of a hike,
but they enjoyed the stroll. Not so in this weather, however.
The cold didn't bother him, and Isla promised it didn't bother
her either, but each time he gave in, her lips were nearly blue
by the time they arrived. He wasn't giving her that option
today.

The ride to the castle took only a few minutes. They
parked next to the other vehicles and got out. The sound of
Christmas music could be heard, even outside. Isla met
Hayden's gaze as they both laughed. The castle was always
chaotic. It couldn't be anything less with so many couples, but
it was always more so during the holidays.

Hayden hurried to the door, holding her so she didn't slip
on the ice. Once inside, they hung up their coats. Isla took the

box from him and made her way upstairs to give it to Marcail, who was obsessed with wrapping. Hayden had to admit that he always looked forward to seeing what she created. However, some of the presents were so pretty he didn't want to open them.

He didn't care what decorations they put up, but Isla liked his input, so he made sure he always gave her his opinion. This year, he had selected the copper, alongside Isla's choice of teal, which he had to admit, looked amazing on their flocked tree. From now on, he would do more than nod to Isla when she threw out colors.

Hayden's eyes followed Isla up the stairs, lingering on the sway of her hips encased in the pants that molded to her beautiful body. He loved her in those jeans, and he knew she had worn them with the charcoal gray jumper for that reason. Only when she was out of sight did he look around. The great hall was aglow with all the Christmas lights.

Garland hung over every door and window—and everywhere else the girls could find a place for it. The twenty-four-foot tree stood off to the side, drenched in neutral colors, pinecones, popcorn, cranberries, and dried fruit strung together. The girls had called it *cottagecore*. He thought it looked like they'd decorated by taking a trip into the woods. Regardless, he quite liked the outcome.

Hayden spotted Galen exiting the kitchen with the largest cookie Hayden had ever seen. He called out to his friend. Galen nodded as he chewed and made his way over.

"Made just for me," Galen said around a crumbly mouthful.

Hayden chuckled. "It's to keep you out of the kitchen for a wee bit."

"I know," he replied with a grin. "That's why I like it."

"I need to talk to you about something." Hayden explained about Dale while Galen ate.

Galen shrugged when he finished. "I think it's a good idea to invite him. Want me to help you talk to the others?"

"Aye. That'll make things go faster. Thanks."

Hayden slapped him on the back and smiled as they headed in different directions. By the time Isla returned, he'd already spoken to Ian and Broc. When Hayden saw her, he walked to Isla. "Galen, Ian, and Broc are good with Dale coming. Galen is helping me query everyone."

"Really?" she asked, her eyes lighting up.

Hayden wrapped an arm around her shoulders and led her to the kitchen. "That's only three of us."

"Four, including you."

"Five. You're forgetting yourself. It isna just the Warriors who need to agree to this. It's everyone."

She beamed up at him. "You're pretty wonderful."

"I know," he said with a wink.

In the kitchen, he snagged a mini-tart that sat cooling on the island and bit into it. He groaned at the amazing taste of the roast beef and Gruyère. Isla wiped some of the crumbs from his lips. He tipped his chin up at the wine fridge, and Isla nodded with a grin. They loved to sit before the hearth in the great hall after it had been decorated, and they hadn't had a chance to do that yet.

She got a bottle of wine as she spoke to Reaghan, Saffron, and Larena, who had done the baking for the day. Hayden chuckled as he watched the trio toss flour at each other. Isla ducked out of the way just in time. She got two glasses as he piled tarts on a plate and slipped out of the kitchen before they caught him.

By the time Isla joined him, he was situated in one of the two chairs. Hayden handed Isla a tart and opened the wine. After it had been poured, they clinked their glasses together.

"To family," he said.

Isla smiled, her eyes tearing up. "To family."

No matter what, he would convince everyone to invite Dale. And if he had to go to Dale himself, he would make damn sure the Warrior was at the solstice. Because that's what his wife wanted.

"I love you," she said.

He leaned over and kissed her. "I love you."

They settled back in the chairs with nothing but the lights from the tree, garland, and the blaze in the hearth lighting the room. With the music blaring, he took stock of his family and felt gratitude and love fill him.

Isla slid her hand into his and smiled. Hayden grabbed another tart. It would be a great holiday.

ROAST BEEF AND GRUYÈRE MINI-TARTS

<u>SERVINGS:</u>

12 servings

<u>INGREDIENTS:</u>

- 12 prepared mini-tart shells
- About 7 oz of thinly sliced roast beef
- 1 tablespoon butter
- 1 shallot, diced
- 1 cup shiitake mushrooms, thinly sliced
- 1 tablespoon fresh thyme, chopped
- ¼ cup cream cheese, room temperature
- 1 egg, room temperature
- 1 tablespoon horseradish
- 1 cup Gruyère cheese, grated
- Salt and pepper to taste

<u>**INSTRUCTIONS:**</u>

1. Preheat oven to 375°F. Remove mini-tart shells from freezer and place on a parchment-lined baking sheet. Place a small mound of the sliced roast beef into each cup.
2. Heat a medium skillet over medium-high heat. Melt butter, then add shallots and mushrooms. Add thyme, salt, and pepper and then sauté until browned. Remove from heat. Spoon mushrooms onto roast beef.
3. Place cream cheese and egg into a small bowl and whisk until smooth. Season with a pinch of salt and pepper. Spoon into tart shells, allowing the mixture to settle into them.
4. Sprinkle each cup with some grated cheese before transferring to the oven to bake for 20 minutes. Cool for 5 minutes before serving.

GALEN AND REAGHAN

Reaghan smiled when she felt familiar arms wrap around her. Galen nuzzled her neck, making her smile.

"You smell like cookies," he murmured.

She couldn't help but laugh. No matter how much Galen ate, he was always hungry. "That's your stomach talking."

He slowly ran his lips up to her hairline at the back of her neck. "Mmm. I disagree."

"I'm covered in flour," she warned.

His chest rumbled as he chuckled. "When has that ever bothered me?"

Reaghan turned to face him, his deep blue eyes locked on her. She tucked a strand of dark blond hair that had fallen into his face behind his ear. "I need to clean up."

"Where are the others?"

"They were here early this morning, well before me. So, I told them I'd clean."

Galen gave her a quick kiss on the lips. "I'll help."

Reaghan walked to the sink as Galen began putting away all the treats they'd baked. She glanced at him just in time to see him pop a cookie into his mouth. "Try not to eat everything."

He just winked at her in response. "Hayden and Isla want to invite Dale to the solstice."

"Dale? Really?" Reaghan asked in surprise.

"You doona agree?"

"It's not that," she told him as she scrubbed a pan. "I just hadn't thought about him in a long time. Which, now that I say it, sounds horrible."

Galen set aside a container of cookies and reached for an empty tin. "It isna, babe. And I doubt you're the only one."

She paused and looked at her husband. "Have you thought about him?"

"Aye. On occasion."

"You never said anything."

He glanced up and shrugged. "What's there to say? He fought against us. He chose his side."

"Some might say that he didn't really have a choice."

"Some," Galen said in a soft voice.

Reaghan stopped washing and turned toward him. He blew out a breath and lifted his gaze to her. "Tell me," she urged when she saw him struggling.

Galen shrugged. "If things had gone differently for him, he could've joined us. If things had gone differently for me or any Warrior here, we could've ended up in his shoes."

"You can't think like that. Everything happened the way it was supposed to."

"Maybe. Yet, it was Isla who brought this up to Hayden. It should've been one of us."

Reaghan shook her head. "It doesn't matter who thought about it. What matters is that we're talking about it now."

"I know." Galen went back to packing the food.

Reaghan returned to her washing, but she couldn't stop thinking about Dale. Had they been wrong not to reach out years ago? He'd been their enemy but he wasn't now. At least, she hoped not. There were plenty of *droughs* around who could step into the shoes of ones like Deirdre, Declan, and Jason, those who had endeavored to control the Warriors for power. Who was to say that Dale wouldn't join forces with one of them? Especially with things happening on the Isle of Skye with the Druids.

"What do you think about Dale joining us?" Galen asked.

Reaghan rinsed a pan and set it aside to drain. "Usually, after we vanquish an enemy, they're not around for us to consider such a thing."

"Exactly. He might be a Warrior, but he fought all of us at the castle. No' just the Warriors."

"If I've learned anything throughout my life, it's that everyone deserves a second chance." She met Galen's dark blue eyes and smiled softly. "Everyone. I agree that he should be invited."

Galen grinned as he walked over and kissed her gently. "Always the voice of wisdom."

"Don't you forget it."

"Doona worry, babe. You willna let me."

Reaghan threw a handful of water on him.

"Och, lass. You doona want to get into a water-throwing war with me. Remember what happened last time?"

Oh, did she ever. It had been a decadent night of hedonism.

"You keep looking at me like that, and I willna be responsible for what happens next," he warned, his eyes darkening with need.

Reaghan heard a bout of laughter come through the kitchen door, a reminder that they weren't at home but at the castle. Regretfully, she turned back to the dishes. "Later."

"A promise I intend to make you keep."

"Without a doubt," she said, glancing over her shoulder at him.

She returned to the washing, her thoughts on the happiness that those at the castle had found throughout the years. While she knew that Galen and the other Warriors had kept tabs on Dale, as she'd said, she hadn't thought of him in years. As long as he wasn't making trouble for anyone, she hadn't cared. She hadn't thought about what his life might be like or if he'd had trouble adjusting after Jason's defeat. She hadn't wondered if he'd had somewhere to go or anyone who could help him.

There had finally been peace for the Warriors and Druids at MacLeod Castle, and that was all she had cared about. But she should have been concerned for Dale. He had eventually found his way, but it wasn't because of any of them. They had left him to his own devices, and he could've just as easily returned to evil.

If he had, the blame could have—and *would* have—been

laid at their feet. Everyone at the castle knew firsthand how difficult it was for the Warriors to remain in control of the gods within them. They, of anyone, should have lent Dale a hand. He might not have taken it, but they should've offered regardless. And the Druids should've helped.

Reaghan finished the last of the dishes and rinsed the sink before reaching for a towel, only to find that Galen was already drying. "I didn't know you were there."

"You were deep in thought."

She shrugged. "Hard not to be."

Galen tugged on an auburn curl that'd escaped Reaghan's ponytail. "I understand."

"Reading my mind without warning me isn't nice," she scolded.

After so many centuries, he had perfected his mind-reading power, but he made sure not to use it on those closest to him unless he felt it was needed. "I wanted to make sure you were all right."

"I am."

"Your thoughts say otherwise."

She shrugged and began wiping down the counters and island. "It's difficult not to think about what we failed to do for Dale."

"You know we've always kept an eye on him. Just in case."

"I know. Though it's not like we talk about him. Ever."

Galen realized that might not have been the right move. "We do."

"You mean the Warriors?" she said, her head snapping up.

He searched her gray eyes and nodded. "Until there was a reason to talk about him, it was decided that—"

"That the women didn't need to know," she said over him.

Galen wrinkled his nose at how that sounded coming from her lips. "We had good intentions."

"Men," she said in exasperation. "How many times do we have to tell you that we're perfectly capable of handling things? We don't need you to shield us from everything."

"Aye, babe, maybe no', but we're protectors by nature. It's what we do."

A wet towel hit him in the side of the head. Galen shook it off to find Reaghan with her hands on her hips and fire in her eyes as she glared.

"Do. Not. Try. That," she bit out.

But he knew he had already won. "Try what?" he asked innocently. He set aside the last pan and spread out the towel to dry before bending to retrieve the one his wife had thrown at him. He placed it next to his and faced her. "You fell in love with a Warrior. You knew what you were getting into."

"Did I?" she retorted icily, but the light in her eyes danced. "I don't think I did."

He took a slow step toward her. "Should I remind you? I know just where to touch to make you melt."

"And I know where to touch you."

His balls tightened in anticipation. He took another step. "Aye. You do."

Her pulse jumped wildly in her throat. Galen bit back his

grin as he came within reaching distance of her. Reaghan suddenly turned and raced from the kitchen. He smiled before running after her. Her playful shriek filled the hall as she made for the stairs. Galen rushed past the others, ignoring someone calling his name as he raced after his wife.

Reaghan glanced over her shoulder at him, a smile on her beautiful lips. He jumped to the second floor, landing as she reached the top. He snatched her to him and hoisted her over one shoulder.

"Galen!" she shouted over the music and playfully hit his back. "Put me down. You cheated."

"It isna cheating if you run from him!" Hayden shouted after them.

Galen lifted a hand of thanks to him and strode down the hall to the rooms they kept at the castle. He kicked the door shut behind them and tossed his wife onto the bed, following quickly to cover her body with his.

She reached for him and pulled his full weight atop her. "Mmm. The feel of you gets me every time."

He gripped her hip with one hand and ground into her softness. It didn't matter how many centuries passed, he never tired of this woman. She was part of him. His heart, his soul. His very essence. The passion between them had been unmistakable from the beginning, and it never let up.

"You're the reason I'm the man I am," he whispered.

She cupped his face, her eyes soft and full of love. "You were already a good man, my love. But we make a great team. Individually, we are strong. Together, however, we're formidable."

"Oh, aye." He bent and placed his lips on hers, lingering. "I love you more than you'll ever know."

"Show me," she said, her voice rough with need.

Galen slipped his hand under her jumper and took her mouth in a heated kiss.

SPICY POMEGRANATE MOSCOW MULE

FOR A SINGLE GLASS:
INGREDIENTS:

- 2 oz vodka (brand of choice)
- Juice from ½ a lime
- Juice from ¼ of a small grapefruit—plus slices for serving
- 1/3 cup pomegranate juice
- 1-2 jalapeño slices
- Ginger beer for topping
- Pomegranate arils and fresh mint for serving

INSTRUCTIONS:

1. Fill a cocktail glass with ice.

2. Combine the vodka, lime juice, grapefruit juice, pomegranate juice, and jalapeños in a cocktail shaker.
3. Fill with ice and shake until combined - about 1 minute.
4. Strain into your prepared glass.
5. Top with ginger beer.
6. Garnish as desired.

FOR A PITCHER:
INGREDIENTS:

- 1 cup vodka (brand of choice)
- Juice of 2 limes (about ½ cup)
- Juice of a small grapefruit (about ½ cup)
- 1 1/3 cups pomegranate juice
- 1 jalapeño, sliced
- Ginger beer for topping
- Pomegranate arils and fresh mint for serving

INSTRUCTIONS:

1. Combine the vodka, lime juice, grapefruit juice, pomegranate juice, and jalapeños in a large pitcher. Stir to combine.
2. Chill for 2 hours. The longer the jalapeños sit, the spicier the drink.
3. Strain out the jalapeños and discard.
4. Return the drink to the pitcher and chill until ready to serve.

5. When ready to serve, fill the pitcher with ice and
   top off with ginger beer. Or fill glasses with the
   spicy mix and top each glass with the ginger beer.

BROC AND SONYA

"Rummy," Sonya said as she laid down her last card.

Broc grinned from across the table as Arran and Veronica looked at the cards still left in their hands. "That puts Sonya with the most points," he said as he tallied their games.

Arran counted the cards he had left and gave the total to Broc. Then he glanced at Sonya. "You're on a winning streak."

"Tell me about it," Ronnie said as she glanced at the notepad that put her dead last. She drank the last of her wine. "I think I need a refill. Anyone else?"

Broc shook his head. "I'm good, thanks."

"Not me," Sonya replied.

Arran got to his feet. "I'll come with you. I want to see what's left over from lunch."

"No," Ronnie said as she pushed back her chair. "You want to see if you can find more strawberry scones."

Arran chuckled. "Yep."

Sonya waited until the couple was gone before putting her foot atop Broc's leg under the table. He immediately placed his hand over her bare ankle, knowing that she was cold.

"It would help if you wore socks. Or boots," he told her.

She shrugged. "They didn't go with the outfit."

"Then maybe choose something else to wear."

"Do you know me at all?" she teased.

He rolled his brown eyes and reached into his back pocket. "Oh, aye. I know you so well that I brought socks." He dangled the fuzzy socks with Baby Yoda on them from his thumb and forefinger.

She shouldn't have been surprised. Broc always looked out for her—just as she did him. It was nice knowing that someone was there and knew you better than you knew yourself most times. She couldn't imagine life without him. She didn't even want to try.

He removed the ballet flat from her foot and tugged the sock on before motioning for her to give him her other foot. Within moments, her feet and ankles were warming.

"I should've put some socks in my purse," she said.

"Now that you have the socks and have boots here, how about a walk?"

She grinned and jumped up. "That sounds delightful."

It wasn't long before she was snuggled into her thick coat and scarf. Broc put on a coat, but he didn't button it because the extreme weather didn't bother the Warriors. Then, they walked together from the castle out into the snow.

"There's going to be a thick layer for the solstice," Broc said.

"Something about the fire reflecting off the snow is so pretty."

He squeezed her hand and directed her toward the trees. "I have to agree."

They walked in silence, listening to the snow fall. It wasn't until they reached the woods that she released him and stood among the tall trees with her eyes closed. She didn't need to be near them to hear what they said, but standing with the trees always soothed her in ways she couldn't quite put into words.

She had heard the trees from the time she was a small child. Their whispers and greetings. Their warnings. They had saved her many times. Now, as they stood like silent sentries with the snow piling atop their branches, she felt their contentment and delight. Few knew that everything had a voice, even trees. Not everyone could hear those whispers, but a select few could.

The trees loved every season. The spring meant new growth, new life. Summer was filled with abundance. Fall came with shedding the old. And winter brought the snow. The trees loved how it tickled their bark and piled higher and higher on their branches.

When she opened her eyes, she saw that Broc watched her. A muscle in his cheek moved, making her notice his incredible jawline and his handsome face that still made her stomach flutter. His nostrils flared.

"I love watching you listening to them," he said tenderly.

She removed a glove and took his hand to place it on a tree, then covered it with hers. "Close your eyes."

"You know I can no' hear them."

"Trust me." He did as she asked. Then softly, she said, "Listen to the silence. In it, you'll feel them. They don't shiver as we do. They stand tall and proud while providing shelter for others. Their limbs remain sturdy and strong, no matter how much snow and ice form. They welcome each season and the changes they bring." She studied his face, watching as the furrow in his brow eased, and his lips curved into a slight smile. "You feel it."

"I...do."

"Everyone who tries can feel them. You don't need to hear their words to sense their emotions."

Broc's dark eyes opened as he smiled at her. "I wish I could hear them."

"I wish you could, too."

"What are they saying now?"

It was her turn to grin. "They welcome us. They're glad we're here, walking among them when so many ignore them during the long, dark winter."

"But no' you."

"There is pleasure to be found in the woods, no matter the season. Rain or shine. Hot or cold. The trees are there, waiting to share their wonders with us."

Broc pulled her against him. "You're a marvel."

"I'm just me."

"Like I said. A marvel."

She buried her hands beneath his coat. "So are you. The only Warrior with wings. I love watching you fly."

"We've come a long way from where we were when we first met."

"We've still got a long way to go."

He kissed her forehead. "I love the sound of that."

She rested her cheek against his chest and listened to his heartbeat. "More dangers are coming."

"Did the trees tell you that?"

"They've been uneasy since the incident with the Ancients."

Broc held Sonya a little tighter. The Ancients were Druids who had long left the mortal world. They chose who and when they spoke. If they ever spoke, they did so in riddles. While none of the Druids could call them up at will, the Ancients spoke to Isla most of all. Yet it wasn't that long ago that every Druid at MacLeod Castle had heard the Ancients' shouts before they suddenly went silent.

And they'd been quiet ever since.

The longer that continued, the more Broc was convinced that something was very, very wrong. The Ancients were extremely powerful entities. He wasn't sure anyone could call them spirits since they never took form, but it seemed they were always there. He didn't know anything that could do them harm. And it wasn't unlike them not to answer any of the Druids. Sonya had told him repeatedly that there was nothing to worry about, but he saw the concern growing in her amber eyes.

"Do the trees know what happened that night with the Ancients?" It wasn't the first time he'd asked the question, and he hoped that one day the trees might tell Sonya something.

She shook her head of curly red hair. "Nothing."

"But they're troubled?"

"That night rattled the world," she said as she lifted her head to look at him. "It wasn't only us who heard the Ancients. The Skye Druids did, as well. And I bet if we asked, we'd discover that every Druid did. Not to mention the plants. Animals. Everything heard and felt it."

Broc brushed snow from her cheek. "Which isna something that's happened before."

"Not that we know of. The Ancients have always been around. We don't know their reasoning for anything. We can only speculate."

"I doona have a good feeling about it."

"None of us does, honey. But what can we do?"

He shrugged and turned Sonya to press her against a tree. "I think we need to try something. Anything."

"I agree. I'm just not sure what. We can't make the Ancients talk if they don't want to."

"What if something happened to them?"

Her brow furrowed. "What do you mean? They're the Ancients. What could possibly happen to them?"

"I doona know. It was just a question." But it had obviously upset her. He decided to turn the conversation for now. Broc looked at the tree limbs overhead. "I never would've guessed they enjoyed winter."

She grinned, the lines of worry easing from her face. "They provide so very much for so many. They're incredible."

"Do they get lonely when there isna someone like you near to hear them?"

"They talk to each other."

He gazed down at her. "We will do our part to protect as many of them as we can."

"That's one of the many reasons I love you." She beamed up at him.

Broc tugged out her glove and helped her put it on. Her nose was turning red, which meant it was time to return to the warmth of the castle. They headed toward the gigantic stone structure on the cliffs with the sea beyond. It had been their home for many years before they built their own place deep in the forest.

"There's nothing better than being with family," Sonya said.

He smiled as he glanced at her. "It is my favorite time of year. It might be loud and chaotic, but I wouldna want it any other way."

"Hmm. Agreed. What we have here at the castle is something extraordinary. We could've moved on from each other and gone our separate ways, but I'm glad we didn't."

"We're a family. An unconventional one, but a family all the same."

She leaned her head against his arm as they made their way back to the castle.

Broc looked upward. The thick clouds hid the sun.

"I'm not that cold."

He jerked his head toward Sonya. "What?"

"You want to fly," she said with a grin. "I know that look of yours."

Broc hesitated. "You're already chilled."

"I'm never too cold for that."

He grinned and called to the god inside him as his skin

turned indigo. Talons extended from his fingers, fangs filled his mouth, and wings tore through his sweater and coat.

Sonya sighed. "You could've removed them first."

"What's the fun in that?" He shed his ruined clothes and gathered her into his arms before unfurling his wings.

When he jumped into the air and started to fly, Sonya's smile was bright. He flew them around the castle and out over the sea. When he felt a tremor go through her, he turned and made for the castle. A large bed piled with warm blankets and a fire awaited them. He felt her gaze and looked at her. They shared a smile as he landed atop the battlements. He didn't release her as he made his way into the castle and to their room, where he intended to spend the rest of the day warming her.

CINNAMON CREAM CHEESE COOKIES

COOK TIME:

Prep: 10 min
Cook: 10 min
Total: 20 min

SERVING:

Approximately 28 cookies

INGREDIENTS:

- 1 stick unsalted butter, softened
- 4 oz cream cheese, softened
- 1 ½ cup powdered sugar
- 1 egg, room temperature
- ½ teaspoon baking powder
- 1 teaspoon vanilla bean paste or extract

- Pinch of salt
- 1 ¾ cup all-purpose flour
- ¼ cup granulated sugar
- 1 tablespoon ground cinnamon

<u>INSTRUCTIONS:</u>

1. In a large bowl, cream the butter and cream cheese with a hand mixer until smooth. Gradually add the powdered sugar until combined. Add egg, baking powder, vanilla, and salt. Mix to combine. Add flour slowly until fully incorporated, scraping the sides as needed. Place in fridge for one hour to rest. Dough needs to be chilled before baking. DO NOT skip this step.
2. Preheat oven to 375°F. In a small bowl, mix the cinnamon and sugar. Set aside.
3. Roll dough into 1-inch-sized balls (about 2 teaspoons worth of dough). Roll until coated in the cinnamon-sugar mixture. Place on a parchment-lined cookie sheet (to reduce spreading) about 2 inches apart.
4. Bake for 8-9 minutes until just set. Do not overbake. It is hard to tell when these cookies are ready. They will puff up but won't get golden brown. Let cool on baking sheet for 10 minutes. Transfer cookies to a wire rack and let cool completely.

LOGAN AND GWYNN

Logan reclined naked on the bed, propped against the headboard, his arm tucked behind his head as Gwynn paced before the fire with only a blanket wrapped around her.

She glanced at him and sighed loudly. "I've got nothing. Nada. Not one. Single. Thing."

"There's still time."

"Time?" she repeated shrilly in her Texas accent as she halted and shot him an incredulous look with her violet eyes. "I have no time, baby. I'm *out* of time."

Logan licked his lips to keep his smile hidden. He knew better than to tease Gwynn when she was in this kind of mood. She never found it funny, and he would likely spend the next few days apologizing. It had taken him a wee bit to realize that, but he'd learned his lesson. "It's just a gift."

"That we're supposed to *make* ourselves," she muttered as she began pacing again. She shook her head of black hair. "I'm not crafty. I have no craft."

It took everything he had not to burst out laughing. Logan bit his tongue to keep his expression passive. It was a good thing, too, because Gwynn looked at him to make sure. He swung his legs over the side of the bed and stood on the plush rug. Even with the remodeling they'd done on the castle, nothing could fully keep the dampness and cold out of the stones.

He crossed the bare stones to the next rug where his wife paced. Logan gently grabbed her shoulders and looked into her stunning eyes that had held him captive from the first moment he'd seen them. "You do this every year. And you think of something every time."

"I'm out of ideas this time. Truly. Tell me again why I can't just buy something off Etsy? No one would know."

"You would."

She let out a dramatic sigh. "I hate when you're right."

Logan felt the chill on her skin and led her back to the bed. They climbed under the covers. Once she was settled against him, he said, "Take a breath, and we'll tackle this."

"Remind me why we don't buy presents for each other anymore?"

"Because it's more personal to give something we've made." What he didn't say was that the idea for these gifts had been hers and Larena's. That wouldn't make the situation better.

She sighed once more. "I'm drawing a blank."

"It isna who it's for, it's what you're making. Try to find something you can create for an individual instead of creating something and gifting it."

"Stop being rational and logical."

This time, he didn't suppress the chuckle. "Only when you need it, darlin'. Now, you know exactly what to get Lucan."

"It was just my luck that I had to draw one of you."

Logan frowned. "I'm trying not to be offended."

"You know what I mean. It's easier to find gifts for women. But Larena just *had* to suggest that everyone's name go in the pot together." She lifted her head to look at him. "Why aren't you complaining about picking Sonya's name?"

"Because a gift is a gift."

"Yes, and it's supposed to be unique for each individual. Not just something someone slaps together and says: '*Here, open it.*'"

He'd hoped that she would reach the conclusion on her own. But as smart as his wife was, she got too lost in a problem at times to see the solution clearly. "What business do you have, beautiful?"

She rolled her eyes and plopped her head back on his chest. "Candle making."

"How successful is said business?"

"You know how much."

"Tell me," he urged.

Gwynn was silent for a moment before grumbling, "Very successful."

"And what do you do periodically throughout the year?"

"Make new scents for the seasons or holidays."

He grinned as he heard her voice lighten as her mind started turning with ideas. "Aye. Now, what could you make Lucan that would be singularly his?"

"His own scent," she said as she sat up with a bright smile. "You really think he'd like that?"

Logan caressed the side of her face, taking in the ethereal beauty that was his Druid wife. "Verra much. I know I love mine."

"You're my husband. You're supposed to say that," she teased.

He pulled her down onto his chest for a slow, leisurely kiss. "You chose the scents that made you think of me. Why would I no' love it? It came from you."

"Keep talking like that, and we won't make dinner."

He settled her on top of him and grinned. "Trust me. Many will no' be sitting down tonight."

"Then I won't feel bad at all."

"Now that your crisis is over, can we focus on me?"

"You?" she asked with a laugh.

He rolled her onto her back and tickled her. "Aye, me."

"Stop." She squealed while laughing.

Logan gave her a few more tickles before he relented. "I'm glad you talked me into staying at the castle tonight."

"It's been some time since we all stayed in our old rooms for more than a night. Cara thought it would be nice to have everyone close before the solstice."

"Makes you think back to when we all lived in such close quarters."

"And hid out in our rooms to get some time alone," she said with a laugh.

He gave her a quick kiss. "The bickering could get out of hand at times."

"The love and the laughter."

"Aye. Family is about all of that."

Gwynn moved a lock of golden brown hair from Logan's face. His warm, hazel eyes stared down at her with such love that it made her breath catch. Loving him and being loved by him was the easiest thing she had ever done. He always knew exactly what to say to calm her when she became irrational.

"Have I told you today how much I love you?" she asked.

One side of his mouth lifted in a smile. "Actually, you have no'."

She cupped his face in her hands. "I love you, my amazing Warrior."

"And I love you, my stunning Druid."

Logan rolled to his side and brought her with him. No matter how much time she spent in Scotland, she couldn't get used to the cold. It seeped into her very bones. Thankfully, he didn't mind snuggling beneath the covers with the fire roaring. And his body heat kept her from becoming frozen.

He held her gently against him as her mind went through the scents she had that she used in her candle business. She had created the Etsy shop as a hobby, but it had taken off to the point where she couldn't make the orders fast enough. Luckily, her friends were always ready to help. She wasn't the only one with a prosperous business, and while they all kept their profits, they also added to the castle's overall pot.

After all, the MacLeods had given everyone a home and provided safety.

It didn't take long for her to come up with a scent that was uniquely Lucan. One she really hoped he would enjoy. Now that she had her gift chosen and in mind and only had to make it, she returned her focus to her husband.

He once more had a hand tucked behind his head as he stared into the fire across the room. She kissed his muscular chest, which made him smile and glance at her.

"What are you making for Sonya?"

Logan's grin widened. "You'll have to wait and see."

"That isn't fair. Give me a hint. You have all kinds of talents, but I'm curious."

"You can no' wait a few days?"

She playfully poked at his ribs. "You know I have no patience for surprises."

"Which is why I'm no' telling you."

"Then perhaps we'll make dinner, after all."

"Oh?" he said and wiggled his fingers. "Is more tickling necessary?"

She snapped her arms to her sides. "Nope."

"Just a wee one?" he taunted.

"You're not funny."

"I'm verra funny."

She tried to tickle him, but it was no use. Logan couldn't be tickled. Not even on the bottom of his feet. She should know. She'd tried every part of his body. "Fine. You don't want to tell me the gift, then don't."

"Good." His smile slipped then.

"What?" she pressed. "Is it about Dale?"

Logan nodded and pulled her down onto his chest once more.

"Are you against it?" she asked.

"Nay. It just got me thinking about how different my life could've been."

She shook her head. "Don't do that. It's useless to waste that kind of time. It didn't happen to you. You're here. With me." She wrapped an arm over his stomach and squeezed. "Right where you belong."

"Exactly where I belong."

Her thoughts remained on the Warrior outcast. "Do you think Dale will come? And what's his wife's name? It starts with an *R*."

"Rennie."

"That's it."

Logan wound a strand of her hair around his finger as he often did when he was thinking. "I doona know."

"Would you, if you were in their place?"

"Good question. What would you want to do?"

"Ugh. I don't know." Gwynn thought about that for a moment. "Maybe I'd agree."

Logan's chest rose as he inhaled. "I'd accept."

"You would? Why?"

"Being a Warrior can be lonely. The loneliest. I credit the fact that all of us had each other to lean on with us becoming as strong as we were and are. If I had remained on my own…I doona know what might have happened."

She kissed his chest and smoothed her hand over his upper body. "You'll never have to be alone again. I'll be beside you. Always."

Logan put a finger beneath her chin to tilt her head back. Then his lips claimed hers in a scorching kiss. Desire swept over them once more as their limbs tangled and need consumed them. They forgot about everything but the pleasure between them.

When Logan slid inside her, Gwynn moaned low in her throat. She wrapped her legs around his waist and began to meet his thrusts. All thoughts fell away as she succumbed to her husband's skillful hands.

JACK FROST WINTER COCKTAIL

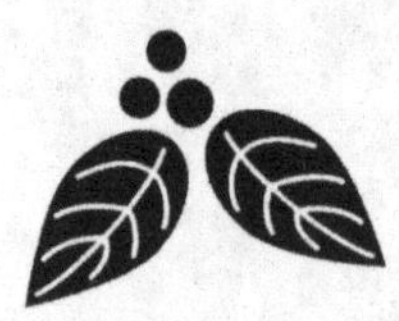

<u>SERVING:</u>
Serves 4

<u>EQUIPMENT:</u>
Blender

<u>INGREDIENTS:</u>

- Light corn syrup for rimming glasses
- 1/3 cup sweetened coconut flakes for rimming glasses
- 3 – 4 cups crushed ice
- 1 cup pineapple juice
- ½ cup Blue Curaçao liqueur
- ½ cup light rum
- ½ cup cream of coconut (not coconut milk)

INSTRUCTIONS:

1. Pour a thin layer of corn syrup onto a shallow plate and the coconut flakes onto a second shallow plate. Dip the rim of the cocktail glass into the syrup and then the coconut flakes. Set aside.
2. In a blender, add the ice, pineapple juice, Blue Curaçao, rum, and cream of coconut. Blend until smooth.
3. Pour the mixture into glasses and serve immediately.

IAN AND DANIELLE

"I love this green. *Stay off the lawn* is the name," Dani said as she swiped the nail polish wand over Ian's toenail.

Ian chuckled but didn't look up from painting her toes. They sat facing each other on the bed, their feet in each other's laps. "I personally like the gold I chose for you. *Enter the Golden Era.*"

"Ooh. Nice name," she said and glanced at the toes he had already painted. "Do you think we should go down after this? I should probably help with dinner."

"We can. I'm sure Hayden and Isla are still by the fire, and Lucan and Cara might come out of the conservatory by then," he said with a smile. "The music has been turned down. My bet is that was Hayden's doing."

That usually meant that most had found their rooms. Dani used the side of her nail to wipe away some polish that got on Ian's skin. She had made sure their day was packed with things to do so hopefully his mind wouldn't turn to his twin—who was now a Dragon King.

The holidays were especially difficult for Ian. While he and Tristan stayed in contact with each other, their duties kept them apart. To make matters worse, Tristan still hadn't recovered all his memories from when he had been Duncan. At least, he had some of them. That was all that mattered to her when it came to Ian.

Her husband's head was bent, showing her the streaks of blond in his light brown hair that she loved to run her fingers through. He changed styles often, constantly trying different looks. Now, his top was on the longer side, while the sides had been trimmed neatly. His sherry-colored eyes lifted to hers.

"I'm being careful," he said with a smile. "Promise."

"You have a steadier hand than I do. I'm not worried."

He eyed her for a moment. "I hope you're staring because I'm too handsome to ignore and no' because you think I'm worrying about Tristan."

"I wouldn't dream of that."

Ian quirked a brow. "Right. I told you yesterday that I was fine. I spoke with him earlier this week."

"And?" she pushed when he didn't elaborate.

He finished a nail and dropped the handle into the nail polish bottle before leaning back and looking at her. "Funny you should ask. Tristan proposed something."

Dani drummed her fingers on his foot. "Why didn't you say anything before?"

"We have our traditions, honey."

"That doesn't mean they can't be changed or altered. He's your twin. One you thought was dead until a few years ago."

The fact that no one—not even the Dragon Kings—knew how Duncan had become one of them was something that no one forgot. When Duncan was found on Dreagan, the Kings hadn't known what to do with him. He had no memory of anything—not even his name. Which was why everyone called him Tristan now.

Ian rubbed his thumb into the arch of her foot just as she liked it. "True."

"If you don't spit it out already, Ian Kerr, I'm going to wax your eyebrows while you sleep."

"I'm a light sleeper. You'd never get it done."

"Oh, you want to test that?" she threatened.

He shook his head. "I'd rather not."

"Smart man. Now, please tell me what Tristan wanted," she begged.

"To get together."

"Perfect. When?"

"Christmas evening."

She shrugged. "I don't see anything wrong with that."

"It willna be just us four."

It took Dani a moment before she realized what he was saying. "Tristan is mated with Samantha, and Sammi's half-sister, Jane, is mated to Banan."

"Aye. Tristan is proposing that the three couples have dinner together."

"They're family. Why not?"

His smile was full of relief. "I was hoping you'd say that."

"Did you really think I wouldn't want to go?"

"I wasna sure."

"He's your brother. I will never say no to us getting together. No matter what."

Ian continued to massage her foot. "I've no' spent much time with Banan or Sammi—or Jane, for that matter."

"Then it's a good time to start. The Kings aren't fighting the Others anymore, and things are relatively calm for the rest of us."

"How long will that last?"

She flicked his little toe. "Don't ask that. Just be grateful for what we have."

"Aye, wife," he said with a wicked grin.

She finished the second coat of polish and reached for the bottle of topcoat. "With Dale being invited to the castle and now this, it's going to be a special season."

"I doona think everyone has given their consent yet about Dale," he cautioned.

Dani waved away his words. "I don't think there will be an issue."

Ian watched her tuck a long strand of silvery blond hair behind her ear. Her emerald eyes were locked on his feet as she meticulously painted his toenails. He had been polishing Dani's toenails for years. She even wanted him to choose the colors more often than not.

The first time they'd polished each other's toes had been when they were both a tad tipsy. It had been so much fun that they did it regularly now. It was intimate and something that was theirs alone.

"Where are we going for this dinner with your brother?" she asked.

Ian applied the second coat to her toes. "Tristan suggested we come to Dreagan, but he said they could come to our home, too."

"Let's go there since this was his idea," she proposed. "Next year, they can come to ours."

"I like that. Good thinking."

She grinned up at him. "I'm good like that."

"More than you know."

Dani blew him a kiss. "Is this a formal event?"

"He didna say."

"Ian, my love, I have to know what to wear. I hate to be over or underdressed."

He laughed, realizing his mistake as soon as she began to talk. "I'll check with him tomorrow."

"Maybe I should call Sammi."

"That would probably be better. It isna like we men obsess over such things."

She snorted loudly. "So, the fact that your closet is full of clothes makes no never mind to you?"

"Precisely," he replied.

"You're impossible."

He screwed the cap on the polish and held out his hand for the topcoat. Dani tossed it to him. He quickly put it on all her toes.

"Should we bring gifts?"

Ian stilled. He hadn't thought of that either.

"I'll bring that up with Sammi and Jane, as well."

He looked at his wife and smiled. "You're the best."

"I know. You can make it up to me with another foot massage."

"Already coming," he said as he set aside the bottle of topcoat. Then he had his hands on her feet again, gently massaging. "Would you want to bring a gift?"

"You know me. I love giving gifts, but not everyone feels the same. It's kinda short notice, so I don't want to put any pressure on them."

Ian frowned. "Them? What about us? That's two gifts. Or four if we buy for each individual."

"Oh, it'd be four," she announced.

Of course, it would, he thought with a smile. "What if we doona say anything to them? What if we bring the gifts just in case? That way, no one gets put on the spot."

"If I bring gifts, I'm going to want to give them."

"Then we do. Right before we leave, so there's no awkwardness for anyone. I doona care if I have anything, but they may feel differently. I suppose you already have ideas for gifts?"

Her grin was huge as she ran both of her thumbs upward along the arch of his foot. "Of course. It wouldn't be much. Just some fun items. I'd see what candles Gwynn has left over from the holiday rush and pick one for both Sammi and Jane. I know that Isla has been obsessed with knitting lately. She keeps making scarves and giving them out, so I would see if there are some of those to add to the candles."

"That would be nice. What about the guys?"

"Well, there is the stash of weapons Hayden has been forging."

"Can I pick them out?"

She nodded. "Absolutely."

"Then it's settled. We'll get that done tomorrow."

"And the gifts to Marcail. I'm so glad she loves to wrap because I hate everything about it."

Ian moved his hands up her legs, shoving the sweatpants upward as he did. "It does make things easier. Our large family can be a lot to take sometimes, but I wouldna want it any other way."

"Me, either. And it looks like our family might be getting even bigger. Before too long, we might be celebrating with all the Dragon Kings."

"Oh, that would be a sight."

Dani settled against the pillows and scooted farther down the bed so he could reach more of her leg. "Do you think they'd ever let us visit Zora? I'm dying to know everything about the new realm. And I confess, I'd love to see dragons flying freely."

"It certainly isna something that would ever happen here. Ask Tristan when we get together."

"I'll do that," she said and moved even closer to him. "Maybe do more of my legs," she coaxed.

He glanced at her toes. "The polish is still wet."

"Then we'll have to repaint them," she said with a seductive smile.

Ian crawled over her and braced his hands on either side of her head as he looked deep into her emerald eyes. "I can no' deny you anything."

"Then strip. Because I want to feel you deep inside me."

He tore his clothes—and then hers—to get them free.

KETO-FRIENDLY PIZZA ROLL-UPS

INGREDIENTS:

- 12 slices of mozzarella cheese
- Pepperoni slices (regular or mini-sized)
- Italian seasoning
- Keto marinara sauce

INSTRUCTIONS:

1. Preheat oven to 400°F.
2. Line a cookie sheet with parchment paper or a baking mat.
3. Lay slices of cheese on baking mat and add pepperoni. Place in the oven for 6 minutes or until cheese slices start to brown on the edges.
4. Remove from oven and allow cheese to cool slightly. Then sprinkle with Italian seasoning.

5. Roll (pin with toothpicks, if needed) and serve with your favorite dipping sauce.

CAMDYN AND SAFFRON

Saffron shouldered open the door to the room. She grinned as she spotted Camdyn reclining on the floor before the hearth where she'd left him. His black head was bent over a sketch pad as he drew. She came up beside her husband and handed him a cup of tea. When he didn't immediately reach for it, she kicked off her slippers and sank onto her knees beside him.

His head whipped to her. "Sorry, sweetheart. I didna hear you."

"I know," she said with a smile.

He shifted on the pile of pillows so she could move more fully onto the rug. Then he set the notebook in her lap as he sipped his tea. "What do you think?"

Saffron put both hands around her mug to warm them, the heat of the fire only helping to comfort her more. She studied the elaborate landscape design on the pad that was now balanced on her legs. "I think you've outdone yourself."

"Really?" he asked, his dark eyes alit with pleasure.

"Absolutely. I think this is your best yet."

He stretched a leg toward the fire as he leaned one elbow on a pillow and looked at her. "I would never have realized how much I enjoyed this if you hadna wanted to redesign our garden."

"Redesign?" she asked with a laugh. "We didn't have a garden. We had weeds and overgrown bushes."

"But it *was* a garden."

She shook her head at him before sipping her spiked chai tea. The bourbon she added created the perfect combination for the holidays. It hadn't taken long for others to try it and fall in love with it just like her—including her husband. "Fine. It was a garden *of sorts*. It's spectacular now."

"Aye," he said, pleased beyond measure at her words.

It helped when his power was controlling earth. That, combined with his skills at designing and then added to Cara's way with plants, and the garden truly was a work of art and a wonderful area for their daughter, Emma, to play. Saffron smiled when she thought of Emma, Bran, and Mallory spending a couple of nights at Dreagan with the Dragon Kings so the adults could celebrate Yule.

Saffron looked again at Camdyn's sketch. She had been attempting to convince him to open his own business since he enjoyed the design part of it so much, but he always reminded her that he couldn't use his power with regular people. And she kept trying to remind *him* that he didn't need to.

For him, however, that was half the fun.

"So, who is this one for?" she asked again. That was when she took a closer look at more than the garden. When she spotted the cliffs, she jerked her eyes to him. "It's for Larena."

"I heard her talking to Cara about wanting to do more on the left side of the castle."

Saffron tossed the pad at him, suddenly suspicious. "You used magic to draw her name, didn't you?"

He hesitated. "Maybe."

"Camdyn!" she cried in disbelief. "We're not supposed to do that."

"It wouldna have been fair to trade with someone."

"Neither is using magic."

He snorted loudly as he sat up. "And you've never used magic to draw someone's name?"

Saffron lifted her chin. "That was different."

"Och, lass. It's the same and you know it."

"It was the perfect gift for Aisley. I knew she'd love it."

"Aye, and this is perfect for Larena."

She rolled her eyes and stuck her still-chilled feet under his leg. "Fine. But we can't do this going forward."

"I make no promises," he replied with a wink. "So, is it the normal downstairs?"

Saffron chuckled as she swallowed another sip of tea. "Exactly. Hayden and Isla are still down there. I heard voices from the game room, though. No sign of anyone else. I'm really glad I didn't start cooking."

"Had you, then everyone would've come down for dinner."

"Maybe. But they wouldn't have wanted to."

He shifted her feet tighter against him. "This is why we agreed on two nights this year. Maybe tomorrow night we'll have the dinner we always miss."

"With two extra settings."

"Aye."

She returned his stare. "Do you know if Fallon has contacted Dale yet?"

"I doona even know if Fallon has been told. I saw him and Larena climbing the outside wall of the castle to their rooms earlier."

Saffron giggled. "What is it about all of us being back here that does that to us?"

"I think it reminds us of the bonds we formed, the victories we achieved over the *droughs*, and the love we discovered."

That made her think of when she had first been brought to the castle. A *drough* had blinded her with his magic so he could use her seer abilities for himself. Saffron had been terrified. After years of blindness, her sight was returned thanks to the Druids at the castle. But she'd found peace and love with Camdyn.

"Doona think of the past," he whispered.

She smiled and shook her head. "Why not? It makes me think of you."

"It took you a long time to break free of the fear that held you."

"I won't ever go back to that again. You helped me see the strength in myself. I know what I survived and came out the other side stronger and more confident than before. I also know another *drough* could come at us again. We're prepared, though."

He gently touched her face with the backs of his knuckles. "Aye. We are."

It was an empty statement. Even in the years of peace, the Warriors and Druids at MacLeod Castle kept training. Because evil never rested, and it never slept. It was always there, waiting for the right moment to strike. Saffron and the other Druids had trained and worked on their battle magic to be ready.

"The past shapes us. Every decision, every action." She set aside her tea and curled against Camdyn. "The past doesn't scare me because I'm here now. My enemies aren't."

Camdyn was constantly amazed at Saffron. She had an inner strength that astounded him every time. What she had endured at the *drough's* hands was horrendous, but it didn't break her. He finished off the tea and placed the empty mug on the floor before sliding down on the pillows and wrapping an arm around her. She moved her long, walnut-colored hair out of the way.

His gaze locked on the orange flames dancing in the hearth. He and Saffron had ended up in this exact spot gazing at the fire so many times over the years. She claimed that he helped her see her strength, but the truth was, *she* was the one who helped him find his way.

No matter what any of the Warriors said, they had all been broken in some way. Some Warriors only found death to ease them. Camdyn had wished for that, as well at times. But that was long before he'd found his brothers at the castle—and well before Saffron.

"Now who is lost in the past?" she said without shifting her head.

Camdyn grinned. "Guilty. I think all this talk of Dale has

me looking back. You're right, though. Parts of my past make me sad, but in the end, everything that happened made me the man I am."

"Regardless of whether Dale comes here or not, I think we're all thinking of the past and everything each of us endured. We celebrated our victories, but we didn't talk about what happened."

"It was over. There wasna a need."

"I think that's where we went wrong. Just because something is over doesn't mean it leaves a person. How long did the nightmares of my blindness haunt me?"

He glanced down to find her tawny eyes focused on him. "Months," he answered.

"I only overcame it by talking them out with you. *We*," she said, motioning her hand between them, "have talked about the past, but have you and any of the others?"

"No' in the way you mean." He sighed and frowned. "I doona think we did it because we were afraid to discuss it. It was more us looking forward and preparing for what would come next."

She blew out a deep breath. "Maybe, if Dale comes, it's time we all sit and talk."

"Lass, he was the enemy."

"*Was* being the operative word," she pointed out.

Camdyn twisted his lips. "What I'm trying to say is that none of us wants to remind him of what he did."

"Or that he fought against us? That he tried to kill each of us?"

"We tried to kill him, too."

Her gaze skated away. "Maybe you're right and talking

now wouldn't be wise. It would be his first time here. But I still believe all of you should talk."

"What about the Druids? All of you fought, as well."

"I'm not leaving us out. Believe me, I know we need to have some discussions, too. I'm going to make sure that happens."

He kissed her forehead. "I know you will." Leave it to his beloved to look out for others. Then he stilled, reminded of her power as a seer. "Did you see something?"

"No. I would've told you," she hurriedly said as she placed her hand over his heart and returned her gaze to the fire. "I can try to see if something comes up."

"Nay. It's almost the solstice. Let's enjoy the time we have. It's never enough as it is."

"Good point." After a long pause, she said, "However, there is something I should've told you last week."

Camdyn waited for her to look at him before he asked, "You had a vision?"

"I did."

If she hadn't come to him immediately, then it hadn't been important. Still, he didn't like that she had kept it to herself. When she bit her bottom lip, his heart clenched. "What is it?"

"I saw myself holding a baby."

"A bairn? O-ours?" He could barely get the words out. They had discussed it, but that was all they had done.

She shrugged. "I just saw the babe in my arms as it looked up at me. It could be ours, or it could be someone else's. That's all I saw in my vision. And before you ask, yes, I tried to look deeper and expand the area to find out more, but there was nothing."

Camdyn looked at her stomach and fought not to put his hand over it. The idea of her belly swelling with their child made him giddy—and terrified him at the same time.

"Say something," she urged.

He blinked and returned his gaze to her face. "I doona know what to say."

"What if it *is* our child?"

"Then I'd be overjoyed."

"Does that mean…should we…?"

Her words trailed off, but he knew exactly what she was asking. "We could continue to come up with reasons for why we shouldna bring another child into this world. There will always be something."

"Unfortunately, yes."

"Yet I'm beginning to think if we want another bairn that we should have one."

Her face split into a huge grin as she threw her arms around him. "Oh, Camdyn. I couldn't agree more."

He caught her lips with his for a long, deep kiss. "Might as well start tonight."

Her tawny eyes glowed with desire as she rose on her knees and removed her jumper, quickly followed by her bra. Camdyn gathered her back into his arms and kissed her until she was breathless and begging for more.

SPIKED CHAI TEA

COOK TIME:

Prep: 5 min
Cook: 20 min
Total: 25 min

SERVING:

Serves 4

INGREDIENTS:

- 3 cups hot water
- 4 black tea bags
- 4 green cardamom pods, crushed
- 4 whole allspice berries, crushed
- 4 whole cloves
- 1 star anise

- 2 whole cinnamon sticks
- ½ teaspoon ground nutmeg
- 1 teaspoon ground ginger
- 2 teaspoons vanilla extract
- 3 cups vanilla almond milk
- ¼ cup honey
- ½ cup good quality bourbon

INSTRUCTIONS:

1. In a medium saucepan, combine water, tea bags, vanilla, spices, and ginger. Bring to a boil over medium/high heat before reducing to a simmer.
2. Stir in the almond milk and honey, whisking to combine.
3. Remove from heat and allow to sit for 10 minutes to steep.
4. Strain through a fine mesh sieve to remove the bulk of the spices and the tea bags, making sure that only the liquid remains.
5. Pour into a heat-proof serving pitcher and stir in the bourbon.
6. Enjoy!

NOTES:

It can be made without alcohol.

RAMSEY AND TARA

"Yes!" Tara shouted as her character on the Portal 2 video game won. Her light brown hair bounced as she jumped.

Ramsey cut her a look. "You doona have to rub it in."

"Oh, but I do." She reclined on the sofa and set aside the controller to grab a handful of popcorn. "How many times have you done a victory lap when you've won?"

He finished off his whisky. "I doona know what you mean."

"Ha," she said and threw a piece of popcorn at him.

Ramsey grinned and set down his empty glass. "Another game?"

"Yes." Then her blue-green eyes dimmed. "Wait. Isn't it getting late? Like time for dinner late?"

"I am a wee bit peckish. Let's go check."

They rose and walked from the game room. He waited until they were in the corridor before draping an arm over her shoulders. She moved closer and linked her arm around his waist, hooking her thumb in a belt loop.

"They turned down the music already," Tara said.

He grunted in acknowledgment. When they emerged in the great hall, Ramsey's gaze locked on Hayden and Isla, who were deep in conversation before the massive hearth. A glance toward the conservatory showed that the doors were still shut, which meant Lucan and Cara were inside and didn't want to be disturbed.

Neither he nor Tara said anything until they entered the kitchen. Earlier, amazing tantalizing aromas had drifted from the room, enticing him and everyone else with the treats being cooked. Now, his stomach rumbled.

A sound from the right drew his attention. Ramsey flicked on the lights. Galen crouched before the lower set of cupboards. He held a tin with the lid off in one hand and had a half-eaten cookie between his lips.

"Hungry?" Tara asked with a laugh.

Galen straightened and pushed the rest of the cookie into his mouth. Around it, he said, "Actually, it was Reaghan who wanted a snack. I figured since I was getting her some food, I'd grab something for myself."

"Just leave some for the rest of us," Ramsey replied.

Galen merely grinned. "It's no' my fault if you're too slow in getting the cookies."

"Take as many as you want of those," Tara said as she walked to the fridge. "We hid the bulk of the goodies."

Ramsey busted out laughing at the horror on Galen's face. "You doona have time to look now. You'd better get back with Reaghan's food before she comes looking for you."

"Bloody hell," Galen mumbled as he gathered the items he'd already laid out on the counter and hurried from the kitchen.

Tara put away the tin that Galen had been eating from. "Before you ask, yes, we really did hide food. We have to, babe. Galen is a never-ending pit of hunger. I swear, I have no idea how Reaghan keeps her kitchen stocked."

"She doesna. At least she stopped trying to years ago. Galen goes to the store at least once a day because she refuses to keep buying food."

"Ha. Good for her." Tara turned slowly in the kitchen. "Since there's no lavish meal, what do you want?"

He walked to the pantry and opened the doors to reveal the room behind it. "Let's see what we can find. Do we want a meal?"

"I plan on kicking your arse again in the game," she called.

"That means something we can eat with our fingers."

"And not get on the controllers," she added as she walked into the pantry with him.

He glanced at her and nodded. "Good point."

They rummaged through the shelves of food. Ramsey looked at the bag of Cheetos, but he had seen the way Tara purposefully didn't grab it. They were her favorite, but she couldn't eat just one. No, she ate the entire bag, and since it was the largest size there was, not only would she consume all of it, but there would be orange dust all over the controllers.

"Don't you dare," she warned when she saw him eyeing the cheesy snacks.

He held up his hands before him. "I'm no'."

"Just making sure you don't." After a moment, she said, "There is cheese in the fridge."

"Crackers and cheese?"

Her eyes widened. "And olives?"

"Of course."

She wrinkled her nose. "I'm going to need a bit more than that right now, though."

"There is some roasted chicken left from lunch. We can make a sandwich with the fresh loaf of bread Cara baked. Without the Cheetos," he told her when she started to reach for them.

"Later," she whispered to the bag and walked from the pantry.

It didn't take long for them to make their sandwiches. While he cut the four different kinds of cheese, Tara picked a selection of crackers and emptied the last of the green olives into a shallow bowl. Ramsey put everything on a tray and was about to walk from the kitchen when Tara held up a finger, asking him to wait.

She pulled containers from the fridge and got out some more bowls. He chuckled when he saw the strawberries, raspberries, and blueberries. After returning the fruit to the fridge, she got the can of whipped cream and two bottles of water.

"What?" she asked as she set the bowls on the tray. "I like whipped cream with my fruit."

He merely shook his head and followed her from the kitchen. On their way through the great hall, he spotted Arran and Ronnie in the library. The front door opened, and Laura stumbled inside, followed by Charon.

"Sorry we're late," she said and shook off the snow from her coat before hanging it up. "It's Charon's fault."

"It's no'," Charon said and hiccupped loudly. "Where's the food?"

"Where do you think?" Hayden answered with a laugh.

Laura waved at them and ushered Charon into the kitchen. Ramsey and Tara used the opportunity and left. Back in the game room, they closed the door and set out their food.

Tara didn't waste any time getting the new game going. She took a few bites of her sandwich but found it easier to pick up the cheese cubes. Then, their game was on. Both she and Ramsey were ridiculously competitive in whatever they did, but it never dissolved into a fight. They made sure of that.

She made a wrong decision with her character that she knew would be detrimental to the rest of the game, and she wasn't wrong. That decision allowed Ramsey to get ahead—and stay there. But she wouldn't give up that easily. This game might be new to them both, but they were quick studies.

"I've got this game," Ramsey called before they were halfway through it.

She didn't answer as she made another bad move. "Damn," she growled when her character was nearly killed. Tara managed to come back from that, but there was no way she could beat Ramsey. Her stomach rumbled, and she glanced at the food. She could either eat or play. Then she saw the whipped cream—and a smile formed as she thought of another game they could play.

Ramsey was on his feet, his entire body moving as he turned the controller one way and then the other as if he could crawl through the screen and make the character do what he wanted. Tara used the opportunity to quickly strip out of her clothes. He didn't bat an eye when she grabbed the whipped cream.

"Baby," she called.

"You're no' going to distract me," he warned. "I'm winning."

She cleared her throat and put her hand on her hips as she stood waiting for him to look at her. "Baby. You're really going to want to look my way."

Ramsey did a double-take. Then he dropped the controller and was before her in a split second. He fell to his knees and looked up at her breasts where the whipped cream covered her nipples.

"You minx," he growled, desire burning hotly in his eyes.

She grinned. "I was tired of playing that game. There's another I'd rather play."

"Who am I to refuse you?" he asked with a grin as he leaned forward and closed his mouth around her nipple, sucking deeply.

She dropped her head back with a moan. God, he felt so good. Her sex throbbed with need. As if sensing the urgency, he stood and yanked down his pants before lifting her and pressing her against the wall. Tara wrapped her legs around his waist just as the blunt head of his cock brushed her center.

She looked deeply into his gray eyes as he slid inside her. The breath locked in her throat. He whispered her name before claiming her lips in a passionate, fervent kiss. His hips began to rock. She slid her fingers into the cool strands of his black hair. No matter how often their bodies joined, she couldn't get enough of him. She knew she would never get enough.

Not in this lifetime.

Not in a hundred.

She moaned in regret when his lips left hers. Tara forced open her eyes to find the half-Warrior, half-Druid who had captured her heart watching her.

"You're close." His voice was rough with desire.

Tara couldn't find words, so she nodded. She *was* close to climaxing. All she needed was…

Her thoughts vanished as Ramsey drove into her harder, deeper, the force of it rubbing her against the wall. His fingers dug into her bottom, but she only felt the thick length of him inside her, each thrust pushing her closer and closer to the edge. His name was on her lips when her body stiffened, pulses of pleasure rolling through her, growing and expanding until they consumed her.

Tara opened her eyes to find herself lying on the sofa with Ramsey still inside her, licking the last of the whipped cream from her as the walls of her sex convulsed with the aftereffects of the climax.

"There you are," he said in his sexy voice.

She smiled up at him. "That was amazing."

"How about round two?"

"You're still on round one."

His smile grew as he leisurely pulled out and then pushed back inside her just as slowly. "Is that an aye?"

"Yes," she said breathlessly. "God, yes."

KETO MINI-CHEESECAKES

COOK TIME:

Prep: 10 min
Cook: 1 hr 20 min
Total: 1 hr 30 min

SERVING:

Serves 6

INGREDIENTS:

For Crust:

- ½ cup almond flour
- 1 tablespoon monk fruit
- ¼ teaspoon cinnamon
- Pinch of salt
- 2 tablespoons butter, melted

Cheesecake:

- 8 oz cream cheese, room temperature
- ½ cup monk fruit
- 1 large egg, room temperature
- ½ teaspoon vanilla extract
- ¼ teaspoon salt

INSTRUCTIONS:

1. Preheat oven to 300°F. Grease a 6-cup muffin tin or prepare with cupcake liners and set aside.
2. Make the crust: Combine almond flour, monk fruit, cinnamon, and salt. Stir well to break up any lumps in the almond flour. If you want the crust all the way up the sides of the cheesecake, double the crust's recipe.
3. Add melted butter to the dry ingredients and stir to combine. Using your fingertips, press down to flatten into the bottom of the muffin tin.
4. Bake for 10-15 minutes, until just beginning to brown. Remove and let cool for at least 10 minutes while you make the batter.
5. Batter: In a large mixing bowl, beat the softened cream cheese until smooth. Add the monk fruit, egg, vanilla extract, and salt. Stir together until well combined.
6. Pour the batter on top of the crusts. Bake for 18-20 minutes. Cheesecakes are done when the centers still jiggle when you tap the sides of the pan.

7. Remove from oven. Let cool for 30 minutes, then cover and chill in the refrigerator. Serve with fresh berries and/or whipped cream.

8. If you didn't use cupcake liners, run a thin paring knife around the edge of the cheesecakes to help release them from the muffin pan. If cheesecakes are really stuck, place the bottom of the muffin pan into a sink of hot water for about 15-30 seconds.

ARRAN AND VERONICA

"We should tell the others."

Arran glanced through the open door of the library and then closed it so no one could overhear them. He walked back to his wife. "We will."

Ronnie reverently held the broken gold torque in her hands. She lifted it to look closer at the ends worn by time. "There's more in the cave. I know it."

"I've no doubt there is." If Arran knew one thing about Ronnie, it was that digging in the dirt for historical finds made her the happiest. It was how they'd met—and how they now lived.

She lowered the torque and speared him with her hazel eyes. The light brought out the gold in her irises. "I bet this is from one of Fallon, Lucan, and Quinn's ancestors. I need to clean it properly to get the thousands of years of grime off it so it gleams once more."

"We will."

"Why are you whispering?"

Arran shrugged. "We've always spoken to the brothers before digging on the land. We didna do that today."

"It wasn't as if I expected to find anything."

He quirked a brow. "Really?" he asked sarcastically.

Ronnie wrinkled her nose. "Fine. I always expect to find something." She shoved a strand of wheat-colored hair from her face. "Besides, they told us we could look wherever we wanted on MacLeod land." Her eyes suddenly widened. "You want to use this as your gift."

"I want *you* to use it," he corrected. "You drew Quinn's name. No' me."

"Oh, that's right." She looked at the metal in her hands once more. "I wish I would've found the other piece. But I will. I'll tell Quinn that when I give him this. I can feel the items waiting to be discovered in that cave."

Arran couldn't stop smiling at the excitement in her voice. Her Druid magic allowed her to find magical objects. While the torque didn't hold magic, he had witnessed his wife's ability to sense when artifacts were waiting to be discovered. He believed her when she said there was more.

The cliffs below the castle were riddled with caves—an entire network of them. In the years before Arran met Ronnie, he and the other Warriors had often explored the tunnels. But he hadn't been looking for artifacts then. He wondered how much they had missed during those early times. No doubt he would be spending a lot of time in the caves over the coming months. They were between digs at the moment, which gave them the perfect opportunity.

"I want Dani to touch it and see its history." Ronnie

grabbed a pillow from one of the sofas and placed it on a table before gently lowering the necklace to rest on top.

With a castle full of Druids who all had special abilities, it made things easier sometimes. Though he was always hesitant to ask Dani to use her magic since there was a chance the object could show her terrible things. But he knew better than to remind his wife of that. She was well aware of the consequences if Dani agreed to touch it—as did Dani herself.

Arran took Ronnie's hands in his and pulled her to the sofa. He sat and tugged her down beside him. A moment later, a soft meow could be heard, and Bastet, Larena's black cat, uncurled from her bed near the fire and stretched before making her way to them.

Bright green eyes looked at him before she jumped onto his lap. Arran scratched Bastet under the chin, which was her favorite spot. The cat immediately began to purr. After a few minutes, she turned in a circle and curled up.

"And you say she doesn't like you best," Ronnie said with a snort.

He grinned and stroked the feline's long, soft fur. "I give good scratches."

"I can't argue with that." They shared a smile before Ronnie rested her head on his shoulder. "Are you happy?"

He was shocked at her question. "Verra much so. Are you?"

"Oh, yes."

Arran mulled over the question and couldn't help but wonder if there was more to it. "Have I made you think I was unhappy?"

"Not at all," she replied. "I just wanted to be sure. I look back and reflect on this at certain times of the year. Christmas always makes me examine the things I have. I'm grateful for all of them, but most especially you and our love."

He put an arm around her and held her close. "Aye, *mo chridhe*."

"I love when you call me your heart."

"Because you are." He paused briefly and watched as Bastet stretched across both their laps. "If I'm ever unhappy, I'll let you know."

She lifted her head to look at him, a smile curving her lips. "I will, too."

"I'm grateful for you," he said as he gazed into her expressive eyes.

"We have a great life. Besides battling evil and fighting off those who want to kill us."

Arran chuckled. "Besides that, aye, we do."

"I never thought I'd have anyone like you. You swept me off my feet. Literally."

He thought back to their meeting at the archeological site. "You didna make it easy."

"If you want something badly enough, you have to earn it," she replied with a smile.

"You were worth every second."

They fell into silence, listening to the fire crackle and Bastet purr. They did have a great life. Nothing was set in stone, and it would always be that way, but he would fight for Ronnie and their love. As well as against evil. There were no guarantees. Every day was a gift, and he treasured it. Everyone at the castle knew how lucky they were to have survived.

And that could be taken from them at any second.

But Arran wouldn't think about that. He had Ronnie in his arms, Bastet in his lap, and his family at the castle. It was nearly as perfect as it could get.

Ronnie sank her fingers into Bastet's silky fur. She stared at the cat while thinking about the threat that had been growing. She wasn't the only Druid who'd felt it, but since no one could name it, they hadn't spoken about it. Yet. She planned to bring it up after the holidays. After what'd happened on the Isle of Skye and then the Ancients' silenced screams, she couldn't shake the unease that swelled each day.

At first, she'd thought it was all in her head, but she knew it wasn't. Something was going on. Did it mean that the Warriors and Druids of MacLeod Castle needed to get involved? She couldn't say either way for sure. But if something threatened their fragile and delicate balance, they had to do something.

Arran's shoulders rose as he inhaled deeply. She lifted her head, straightened, and looked at the man who held her heart and protected her with his very life. He had his dark hair shoved away from his chiseled face. Honey-colored eyes turned to her.

"What is it?"

"Can't a wife look at her handsome husband?" she teased.

His answering grin made her heart skip a beat. "Are my clothes in the way?"

She laughed loudly, causing Bastet to lift her head and

glare at them disapprovingly. Ronnie leaned forward and pressed her lips to Arran's. "They're always in the way."

"I can strip," he offered, waggling his eyebrows.

"Tempting. Especially since I know that everyone else is occupied."

"Tempting?" he repeated, confusion in his expression. "Just tempting? I must be losing my touch."

She rolled her eyes at his dramatic words. "You know you're not. We have Bastet. I don't want to disturb her. Do you?"

"I guess no'," he said as he looked at the cat. He caught Ronnie's gaze. "You're no' fooling me, you know."

"What are you talking about?"

"I know you're worried. You and every Druid here. We are, too, just so you know."

She sighed. She should've known that she couldn't keep something like that from Arran. "It isn't that I didn't want to talk to you about it."

"I know why you didna. It's the same reason I've no' brought it up. It's the holidays. A time for joy and celebration." He pulled her closer. "I only wanted you to know that you doona have to carry the burden alone."

"I know." No matter what might be going on in her life, Arran was always there, strong and steady like a standing stone. The world might batter him, but he withstood it all. That gave her the strength to do the same, even when things got too difficult.

"So, can I give you a gift tonight?"

She laughed and shook her head. "It isn't Christmas. It isn't even Christmas Eve."

"You're no' going to actually make me wait, are you?"

From the moment Arran bought her a gift, he wanted to give it to her. There was no waiting for him. He tried to leave hints to make her guess what it might be. When that didn't work, he attempted to trick her into opening the present, but she always stood firm. She liked the surprise, and she even enjoyed seeing the gifts under the tree as the anticipation grew.

Not Arran. He was fine holding off opening his gifts, but he literally couldn't wait to give things to her. He'd grown so impatient in the past that he had opened a gift for her, simply because he'd wanted her to have it right then.

The process they went through every year got progressively worse once December started. By Christmas Eve, Arran was ready to tear into every one of her gifts and just set them all in front of her. As a compromise, she opened one gift the night before Christmas. It took Arran all day to decide which one he wanted her to open. Even then, he would change his mind a dozen times before she finally grabbed one herself.

But she loved the game they played. Arran and the other Warriors hadn't had a normal life. Not just because they were several centuries old, but because most of them had lost their families when their gods were unbound. When Arran found joy in anything, she accepted it for what it was—all of it.

"You know I am going to make you wait," she stated firmly.

"I brought a gift. Just in case." He grinned knowingly. "I think you'll love it."

Ronnie laughed. "I love everything you get me, but we're waiting."

"It can no' wait."

Before she could reply, he gently lifted Bastet off his lap and settled the feline on hers. Then Arran was up and out of the library. Ronnie shifted so the cat could settle more comfortably. As soon as Arran returned, she said, "I'm not opening it, and you'd better not either. No gifts. Not yet. Just a few more days. You can wait."

"Like I said, this can no' wait." He stopped before her with a large box and carefully set it on the floor.

She eyed it, then him. "Where did you have that hiding?"

"Hayden and Isla were watching it for me."

Watching it? He made it sound like it would sprout legs and run off. "No, I'm no—" The words died when she heard something. She frowned, thinking it was her imagination. Then Bastet jumped down and began sniffing the box in earnest.

"Open it," Arran said with a nod, his eyes dancing with excitement.

She heard the noise again. It was unmistakably a meow. A tiny meow. Ronnie had never yanked a ribbon faster. She carefully opened the lid and looked inside to see a solid white fur ball with blue eyes staring up at her. The kitten rose on its hind legs and meowed up at them. Bastet peered over the box to look inside.

"Oh, my God. You're the cutest thing," Ronnie said as she lifted the kitten out of the box and held it against her. The kitten began to purr loudly as it rubbed its head against her chin.

"What do you think of her?" Arran asked.

Ronnie looked at him and leaned forward to kiss him. "She's perfect. Thank you."

"She's young enough that we can train her to go on the digs with us and even walk on a leash."

She held up the kitten before her. "Do you want to come dig with us?"

The kitten meowed, which made them laugh. Bastet jumped up onto the sofa next to Ronnie and sniffed the kitten. Then the kitten squirmed to get down and went to Bastet. The two curled up together on the sofa, and Bastet started licking the new edition.

"Now comes the hard part—naming her."

Arran laughed. "I've no doubt everyone will be happy to give recommendations."

"She's so perfect. And she and Bastet get along, which means bringing her to the castle every time we come." Ronnie smoothed her fingers through his hair. "We'll have to introduce her to Laura and Charon's dogs."

"They love Bastet, so I doona think that'll be an issue. So?" Arran said as he moved the box out of the way and sat on the floor to lean sideways against her legs. "Happy you got to open a gift early?"

She playfully slapped at his arm. "You know I am. I've wanted a kitten for so long."

"I know," he said. "Merry Christmas, *mo chridhe*."

"Merry Christmas, my heart."

DRUNKEN SNOWMAN COCKTAIL

INGREDIENTS:

- ¼ cup white chocolate, melted
- ¼ cup milk chocolate shavings
- 1 pint vanilla ice cream
- 2 cups hot chocolate
- ½ cup Baileys Irish Cream
- 1 cup whipped cream for topping

INSTRUCTIONS:

1. In two separate dishes, pour the melted white chocolate and milk chocolate shavings.
2. Dip the rims of two mugs into the melted white chocolate, followed immediately by the milk chocolate shavings.

3. Add two scoops of ice cream to each mug.
4. Pour the hot chocolate and Baileys on top.
5. Finish with whipped cream and any extra milk chocolate shavings.

CHARON AND LAURA

"We're in," Laura said with a long sigh. The dogs rushed past her and ran to greet Hayden and Isla. Laura removed her coat to hang it on a hook, then took off her boots. Charon leaned against a wall, waiting for her. She went to him and ruffled his dark hair to get the snow off. "Now for some food."

"I'm fine," he said and hiccupped.

She rolled her eyes and turned him to head toward the kitchen. "Not even close, sweetheart."

Once they were in the kitchen, she pulled out a stool at the bar and made sure he was in it before rummaging for food. Laura glanced up when she heard voices and found Isla carrying Sterling, their Scottish terrier. Sterling desperately attempted to lick Isla's face while wagging his tail happily. Hayden followed behind Isla with their West Highland terrier, Jock, who stared adoringly up at him.

"Let me guess," Hayden said with a chuckle as he came up

beside Charon. "You spent the day trying to come up with a new cocktail recipe."

Charon groaned and dropped his head into his hands. "I was sooooo close."

Laura turned with an armful of food that she dumped onto the island before kicking the fridge closed with her foot. "You had fourteen different glasses on the bar when I made us leave."

"I whittled it down from seventy," Charon grumbled.

Isla's eyes widened. "Seventy?"

"And that's why my husband is drunk," Laura stated.

Charon lifted his head. "I'm no' sloshed, love."

Hayden laughed as he set Jock down. "Aye, you are, my friend."

"I was so close," Charon said again.

Laura couldn't stop the smile. After the last two years of coming up with a special drink to celebrate the solstice, Charon had been stumped for weeks. Two days ago, he'd started making cocktails randomly, but he hadn't been happy with any of them. Then, yesterday, he'd been desperate. He hadn't come to bed the night before. Instead, he'd spent the entire night trying to find just the right drink. She kept telling him that he didn't need to do it, but Charon was nothing if not stubborn.

He held up his thumb and forefinger and looked at her with his deep brown eyes. "So close, love."

"Oh. I forgot the box," Laura said and started around the island.

Hayden rose to stop her. "Where is it?"

"In the back of the car."

"I'll get it."

"Thanks," she called after him. Then she returned her gaze to Charon.

Isla put some roasted chicken with some of Cara's baked bread on a plate and shoved it at him. Charon closed his eyes and ate. Laura blew out a breath. Her husband wanted to make the holidays perfect every year. He'd made the first cocktail on a whim, but it had been a huge hit. The second year, he'd planned the cocktail for a month, and it had been another hit. Which, of course, meant he felt he had to outdo both.

"So sorry we're late," Laura told Isla. "I was trying to make it for dinner, but the roads are getting so bad."

Sonya waved away her words. "There was no dinner. As usual, everyone went their separate ways."

Hayden walked in with a large crate full of liquor that Charon brought for those who wanted it. Everyone liked something different, and he never left anyone out. Laura put a bow on each bottle and handed them out.

She saw Hayden eyeing the bottle of Rémy Martin XO brandy. "That's yours. Take it."

"Oh, you guys didn't need to do that," Isla said as she walked to Hayden, but her smile said she was delighted with the bottle.

Hayden slapped Charon on the back before Hayden hugged her. "Thank you both. I think we'll go up and sample this now."

"Have fun," Laura called as the couple left. Sterling and Jock sat at Charon's feet, waiting for crumbs to fall, which she knew Charon purposefully allowed.

He caught her gaze. "I did what you asked me no' to do."

"Oh?" she said as she walked to him and put an arm around him. "What might that be?"

"No' to let creating the drink consume me."

She kissed the side of his face and rested her chin on his shoulder. "I keep telling you that not everything has to be perfect. We've had some of the best times when everything went wrong. Remember the picnic?"

That made him chuckle, his eyes crinkling as he gazed at her. "I forgot to pack food because I was intent on the champagne remaining the perfect temperature until we opened it."

"And I forgot the blanket."

"And the beautiful day turned into a torrential storm that soaked us within seconds."

She laughed, recalling how wonderful it had been. "It was the *best* day."

"I particularly liked that we had the loch all to ourselves."

"Because no one wanted to be out in the weather."

"Aye. We had quite a lot of fun." His eyes heated.

She moved to sit on the stool next to him. "We really did."

"I have an idea," he said, pushing the empty plate away to face her.

"What's that?"

"I fix everyone whatever drink they want."

She leaned forward and wrapped her arms around him. "I like that idea."

"I have another idea."

"Oh?" she asked.

He took her hand and rose. "Follow me."

Charon walked from the kitchen with Laura at his side, their two dogs on their heels. He brought her to the huge, lit tree she had helped to decorate weeks earlier and stood in its soft glow.

"Do you know why I want it to be perfect every year?" he asked.

She looked at him. "Because you're a perfectionist."

He chuckled. "That's part of it." Charon smoothed his hands over her dark, wavy hair and gazed into her moss green eyes. "It's also because I know how precious this life we have is. I know how close I came to losing you. December is your favorite time of year. We watch a Christmas movie nearly every night. We host a large holiday party for the entire town. You go to great lengths to ensure your gifts are personal, so everyone knows you put a lot of thought into them. You deserve the same, love. It's why I try to make it perfect."

"Oh, sweetheart." Her eyes glistened with unshed tears. "The thing is, everything is already perfect. Because you're here with me. You're all I need."

He brushed a tear from her cheek. "Everything I do is for you."

"I love you so much that it sometimes feels as if my heart is about to burst," she said as more tears fell.

She threw her arms around him and buried her face in his neck as he held her. Charon glanced down to see the dogs staring at them, their heads tilted to the side. He grinned, his heart full. He had Laura, the dogs, and his family. And he wouldn't trade any of it.

He leaned back and cupped her face in his hands. Charon

caught her eyes and shot her a smile. "You were worried that we were late, but it looks as if we have the rest of the evening to ourselves."

Laura sniffed, her eyes dancing with merriment. "You have a devious mind, husband. I like it."

"I thought you might. Should we grab some food?"

"Unless you want to come down later?"

Charon snorted and shook his head. "You're right. Better stock up now."

They returned to the kitchen, grabbed some items for themselves and the dogs, and were on their way to the stairs when they heard a commotion by the front door. Charon detoured and spotted Evie.

"Honey, we were no' the last ones," Charon told her.

Evie grinned as Malcolm walked up behind her with his arms loaded down with bags. He bent to release them before turning and going back outside.

"What is all of that?" Laura asked.

Evie bit her lip as she bent to pet the dogs, who rushed around her, trying to get her attention. "Well, I kinda decided to buy presents for a kids' home."

"Then she said we should help more than one," Malcolm said as he returned with even more presents. "So, here we are."

Laura looked at Charon. "That's a good idea. We do something for those in Ferness, but perhaps we should do more."

"Anything you want," he replied with a smile. Charon looked at Malcolm. "Need help?"

"We got it," Evie said.

Laura waved at the couple. "There was no dinner, so help yourselves to whatever is in the kitchen."

"We'll see you two in the morning," Charon called.

When they walked into the bedroom, Laura asked, "Should we have helped them carry in the bags?"

"They declined any help." He set down the food as the dogs found their beds near the hearth. When he straightened, Laura pushed him back onto the bed. As he fell, he caught her hand, pulling her with him. She squealed with delight as he rolled on top of her. "You said something about helping Evie and Mal."

"No, I didn't," she said and tried to pull his head down for a kiss.

Charon made as if he were getting up. "You're right. I should help."

"Charon," Laura called as she gripped him firmly. "Kiss me now."

"Och. Such a bossy lass," he murmured with a half-smile.

She grinned wickedly. "You love it."

"Aye. I do," he whispered just before he kissed her.

HOLLY JOLLY CHRISTMAS CITRUS COCKTAIL

<u>FOR A SINGLE GLASS:</u>
<u>INGREDIENTS:</u>

- 2 oz vodka (brand of choice)
- ½ oz St-Germain elderflower liqueur
- 1/3 cup freshly squeezed clementine or blood orange juice
- Ginger beer for topping
- Pomegranate arils for topping
- 1 sprig fresh thyme

<u>INSTRUCTIONS:</u>

1. Fill a cocktail glass with ice.
2. Add the vodka, elderflower liqueur, and clementine juice. Top with ginger beer. Add the pomegranates and thyme.

3. Enjoy!

FOR A SINGLE PITCHER:
INGREDIENTS:
Serves 4. Can be doubled.

* 1 cup vodka
* ½ cup St-Germain elderflower liqueur
* 1 ½ cups freshly squeezed clementine or blood orange juice
* 2 12-oz ginger beers
* 1 aril from 1 pomegranate
* 4 sprigs of fresh thyme

INSTRUCTIONS:

1. In a large pitcher, combine the vodka, elderflower liqueur, and clementine/blood orange juice. Chill until ready to serve.
2. Just before serving, add ice, ginger beer, and pomegranate arils. Serve garnished with thyme.

PHELAN AND AISLEY

"Your silence is worrying," Aisley said, sitting between Phelan's legs on the bed as he braided her hair. She had been teaching him different plaits for over a year now. His reasoning? Because they might have a daughter someday, and he wanted to be able to do her hair. Aisley loved when Phelan played with her hair. That meant she was always ready and willing when he wanted to practice on her.

He blew out a breath. "I have to concentrate. This inverted fishtail isna exactly simple."

She smiled.

"And my fingers doona move as I need them to," he complained.

Aisley ran her hands along his bare legs that rested on either side of her. "You can say no."

"It isna that."

"Then what is it?" She was getting impatient since they had been discussing the issue all day. The *issue* being whether

Phelan should follow Rhi's suggestion and help the Light and Dark Fae come together to create the Council that would govern both sides.

Phelan held out his hand for the hair tie. Once Aisley had given it to him, he tied off the ends of her hair. "The braid isna bad, but I need more practice."

"It took you a few tries to master the fishtail. Give it some time with the inverted."

He pulled her back to his chest as he reclined against the headboard on the pile of pillows behind him. "It's the same bloody braid."

"Not really. But we both know you're not irritated at the plait."

"Nay. I'm no'."

She looked up at the ceiling, waiting for him to talk. Only a handful of Fae knew who Phelan was. And there were pros and cons to him making himself known. The Fae, in general, weren't exactly accepting of Halflings, which was exactly what Phelan was. Half Fae, half human, and all Warrior. But his Fae side was that of royalty. Not that it mattered much any longer, especially if they formed the Council.

His strong arms came around her, holding her gently but firmly. "Things will change for us if I do this."

"We've talked about that."

"We've guessed," he replied. "We can no' know for sure."

"Rhi wouldn't have asked if she didn't think you could help."

Phelan grunted. "Rhi is on Zora with Con, doing who knows what. She has other concerns."

"Rhi has done enough for the Fae, in my opinion. Let her

and Con have their time together. They deserve it. Besides, they're getting to know their children."

Phelan pressed his cheek against her head. "There was a time I wanted to know the Fae. Then I came to terms with the fact that it was better if they didna know about me."

"Because of Usaeil. She's gone now and no longer a concern."

"There are others like her out there. We both know that."

Aisley reached up and hooked her hands on his arms. "Then don't contact the Fae."

"And if the Council fails and they go to war? The Dragon Kings have already stopped one Fae War. No one will take too kindly to knowing that I was the catalyst."

She sat up and faced him, shifting her legs so they lay on either side of his hips. Aisley looked deep into his blue-gray eyes and brought his face down for a soft kiss. "It wouldn't rest on your shoulders alone. There are those actively opposing and fighting the formation of the Fae council. Their voices are the loudest. Those wanting the Council leaned too heavily on Rhi. That's why she stepped away to begin with. She knew they had to learn to fight for what they want."

"What if they lean too heavily on me?"

"They might."

He raked a hand through his dark locks, shoving the thick strands from his face. "I'm no' sure I want that responsibility."

"Then there's your answer."

"So, you doona want me to help the Fae?"

Aisley barked a laugh and gripped his arms in frustration. "That's your decision."

"Nay, beautiful. It's *ours*. This affects both of us."

"You know I'll support you, whatever you decide."

"I want to know what you think."

Aisley touched her braid, feeling the weave with her fingertips. She had put off giving him her opinion because she'd wanted to see which way he was leaning first. "It's an honor that Rhi asked you to go to the Fae. Obviously, she thinks you can do some good."

"But?" Phelan asked when she paused.

"But…the fact that Rhi stepped away gives me pause. She spoke at length about how crucial it was that the Fae change. And the first step in that is doing away with royalty to have a Council."

"And if it is so important, why did she leave?" Phelan nodded. "I keep thinking about that, too."

Aisley took one of his hands and held it up as she flattened her palm against his and threaded their fingers. "There's a real possibility that the Fae won't welcome you, despite Rhi having invited you. She's not there to introduce you."

"They may no' believe that she asked me for assistance."

"There's that, yes." She shrugged. "On the other hand, the Fae might gladly welcome you. If they do, you'd likely feel obligated to lend support. Because once you're in, you'd be all in. That would take a lot of your time. Things are semi-peaceful at the moment, but what if that changes? We're talking about our world with the Warriors colliding with that of the Fae."

His brow furrowed. "The Fae know about the Warriors."

"They ignore you all. There's a difference."

Phelan's expression hardened. "No' to mention, the Light might accept me, but we both know the Dark never will."

"They'd likely see you as an interloper."

"The odds are great that my appearance might only make things worse."

"There seems to be more cons than items in the pro column."

Phelan looked into Aisley's fawn-colored eyes and twisted his lips. "I think the right choice is for me to stay out of Fae business. My family hid me for a reason. I doona think the Fae need to know about me."

"Or what your blood can do."

No matter how much time had passed, he couldn't think about the healing power of his blood without thinking of being held prisoner by Deirdre all those long years ago. Maybe the memories would no longer feel like a kick in the gut someday. "You brought up a good point, though. What if we're needed on the Isle of Skye again? My place is with you and our family."

"So. Decision made?"

"Decision made," he agreed.

She eyed him, one brow raised. "How do you feel about it?"

Phelan paused and thought it over. He released a breath as his entire body relaxed. "Good. I feel good about it."

"Just what I wanted to hear." She leaned forward, rubbing her bare breasts against his chest. "Perhaps we can get back to our fun?" she asked with a grin.

He laughed. He couldn't help himself. "Whose turn is it?"

"Mine," she said and leaned over to get the remote from the bedside table.

Aisley flipped the long, black length of her braid over her shoulder and shot him a grin as she scrolled through their list of movies. With so much to discuss, they had opted to stay in their rooms at the castle. Aisley had even stocked it beforehand in case their talk went through the day, which it had.

She shot him a grin as she settled between his legs and used him as a backrest. He was mildly surprised when she chose *The Holiday* since it was one of his favorite Christmas movies. Phelan moved Aisley's hair aside and kissed the spot on the back of her neck that always sent shivers down her spine.

"Ooh," she murmured. "Should I not play the movie?"

He licked her earlobe. "I'm no' going to miss out on Cameron Diaz and Kate Winslet."

"As if I want to miss Jude Law."

"I guess that means this waits," he replied between kisses on her neck. Phelan waited to hear her laugh and tease him back, but there was no response. He lifted his head and looked at her.

"I just want to be sure you're happy with your decision."

He smiled and kissed her brow. "It would've never dawned on me to do anything had Rhi no' come to us. It was only because the request came from her that I even considered it at all. I might have Fae blood, but I've never felt part of them. I only would've gone to the Light if I thought there was a chance that I could do some good and that something would come out of my assistance."

"Rhi would argue that something *would* come out of you being there."

Phelan saw the chills on Aisley's skin and moved the down comforter to cover their legs. "That would be Rhi trying to guilt me because *she* feels guilty by no' being there herself."

"Ohhh. Look at you piecing that together," Aisley said with a pleased smile. "I hadn't thought of that, but I think you're right. She can't be two places at once."

"If the Reapers stay out of Fae business, I think a Halfling should, as well." Phelan shrugged one shoulder. "The more I say it, the more I know I've made the right decision."

Aisley grinned. "You agreed to invite Dale a lot quicker than you decided this."

"People change."

"I agree, which is why I voted to invite him and Rennie. I can't wait to meet her. Both of them, actually. Besides, Dale helped save me."

Phelan tugged her head against his chest and kissed the top of it. "You're a good woman, beautiful."

"You're a good man, sexy."

"Does that mean I can watch Kate and Cameron now?"

Aisley laughed and started the movie.

Phelan tightened his whole body around her before he whispered in her ear. "I love you."

"I love you more."

"I love you most."

She turned her head and met his gaze. "Forever and always."

"Forever and always."

EASY CRANBERRY BRIE BITES

COOK TIME:

Prep: 5 min
Cook: 8 min
Total: 13 min

SERVINGS:

15 bites

INGREDIENTS:

- 4 oz Brie cheese
- ½ cup cranberry sauce
- 1.9 oz package frozen mini filo (15 shells)

INSTRUCTIONS:

1. Preheat oven to 350°F.
2. Cut the Brie into ½-inch squares. Rind can be removed if preferred.
3. Place shells on a small parchment-paper-lined baking sheet.
4. Place a Brie square in each shell.
5. Top the Brie with ½ teaspoon of cranberry sauce. (see notes below)
6. Bake for 7-8 minutes. Serve warm or at room temperature.

<u>NOTES:</u>

- MAKE AHEAD: make bites according to directions but do not bake. Place the filled shells back in the tray they came in and cover tightly with plastic wrap. Place the tray back in the box and freeze for up to 3 months. Allow the bites to thaw before baking as directed above.
- Pepper jelly, fig preserves, honey, or your favorite jam or preserves can be substituted for the cranberry sauce.
- You can make a delicious homemade cranberry sauce by combining one cup water, one cup sugar, and a 12-oz bag of fresh cranberries in a saucepan over high heat. Bring to a boil, reduce heat to medium, and cook for 10 minutes. Cool and store covered in the refrigerator for up to 2 weeks.
- You can substitute puff pastry or crescent roll dough for the filo shells. Cut the pastry into small

squares and place into mini-muffin cups. Then,
follow the rest of the recipe. You may need to add a
few minutes to the cooking time.

- Leftovers can be stored covered in the refrigerator
for 2 to 3 days. To reheat, place them in a 350°F
oven for a few minutes. <u>Do not</u> reheat in the
microwave.

MALCOLM AND EVIE

Malcolm stared at the pile of bags filled with presents for needy children of all ages.

"Marcail is going to kill me," Evie murmured as she stood beside him.

He chuckled and wrapped an arm around her. "She might when she realizes a second load is coming tomorrow."

"I'll help her."

"You forget that she loves to wrap."

"Maybe a few, but not hundreds." Evie looked up at him with her blue eyes. "I overdid it, didn't I?"

He shifted so they faced each other and pulled her against him. "It's the holidays, and thousands of children are without families or anyone to spend these days with. What's one gift?"

"Using my words against me," she said with a shrewd nod. "I should've seen that coming."

He kissed her and looked at the packages again. "Perhaps we should help Marcail."

"If you're offering, then I know we bought a lot." She sighed loudly. "I'm just worried the gifts won't get everywhere in time."

"Let me worry about that."

Her eyes lit up. "You have an idea?"

"I do."

She moved out of his arms and yanked her brown curls away from her face to clip them at the back of her head. He didn't know where the clip had come from, and he had given up trying to decipher how she always had something to use for her hair a long time ago. He couldn't get enough of the length and feel of the curls in his hands and spread out on the pillow beside him.

"Should we lug the bags upstairs?" Evie asked.

Malcolm took her hand and tugged her toward the kitchen. "It's been a long day after an arduous drive—in the snow, I might add. Everyone else has gone to their chambers. Which means…"

"We have the kitchen to ourselves." Evie squealed softly and rushed past him to dig in the cabinets and pantry for sweets and other fare.

He stood to the side and watched. It was safer that way. Evie had a major sweet tooth, and when she was stressed, it got even worse. Malcolm had made the mistake of thinking that he could share her coconut cookies once. He'd nearly lost his hand.

The bliss on Evie's face when she found the container of cheesecake bites made him smile. She had her eyes closed as she ate first one and then a second. Only after she'd swallowed the second did she look at him and point at the treats.

"Want one?" she asked.

He made his way to the bacon-wrapped, cream-cheese-stuffed jalapeños. "I've been waiting for these all day."

"We can't eat them all," Evie whispered as she glanced at the door. "They've been cooking and baking all day, and I wasn't here to help."

"We won't eat them all."

She glanced at the cheesecake bites. "You might have to take these away from me."

"No' happening, darlin'."

"But…I'll eat them all. You know I'll be all grumbly and annoyed that I ate so much sugar at once. Not to mention the guilt I'll feel for not leaving any for the others."

He held out the plate of jalapeños. "Have one of these."

"I'd rather not have my mouth on fire, thank you very much," she stated flatly.

Malcolm looked around. "There's food everywhere. Just put the lid on those and find something else."

"But these are…so good," she said, looking longingly at the bites.

Malcolm called her name and slowly said, "Put the lid on the container and step away."

"I should." Yet she ate another one.

He shook his head and grabbed another jalapeño before searching for something else. As soon as he saw the cold roasted chicken, it made him think of the late-night snacks they used to have when they lived at the castle.

"I knew you wouldn't be able to resist that," Evie said.

Malcolm tore off a piece of chicken and held it out to her. "It's better than sugar."

"Just so we're clear, nothing is better than sugar. However," she said as she set aside the cheesecakes and walked to him. "I do love this roasted chicken."

They ate at the island in silence. He finished first and washed his hands before bringing Evie a towel. While she cleaned up, he put everything away. He turned around to find her leaning back against the sink, her hands on the counter.

"I need to thank you for stopping me from eating all that sugar," she said with a sly grin.

He made his way to her. "We both know you hyped up on sugar isna the way to sleep."

"Who said anything about sleeping?"

"Oh." Now, it was his turn to grin. "You think you know what I want?"

She looked at the ceiling for a moment. "I'm fairly certain I know exactly what you want."

"What is that?"

"Me, of course. You can't get enough of me."

He saw the teasing in her eyes, but her words were all truth. "Is that so?"

"If you can catch me."

She was out of the kitchen before he knew what had happened. Malcolm smiled slowly and took his time turning off all the lights before walking from the kitchen. He stood in the great hall and listened for his wife. The last place she would go would be their rooms, which meant she could be anywhere in the castle.

His enhanced hearing told him that she was to his left. As he concentrated, he made out the sound of her boots on the stone steps. She was going to one of the towers. He jumped to the second floor and walked to the stairs that led up to where he thought she'd gone. When he listened again, he heard only silence.

"You're getting good, darlin'," he whispered with a smile.

Evie shivered in the chilly tower, but she wouldn't be cold for long. She stood in the middle of the room and waited. Their game was also training—just in case. Because evil never slept. She wanted to be prepared in case they had to fight anything with enhanced senses. So, she'd learned to walk silently—or as quietly as one could when running.

Part of the exercise was to see if she could determine where Malcolm was on his hunt to locate her. He always found her. Most times, there was battle training once he did, but she had other things on her mind tonight. She waited, listening intently. She couldn't hear the way he and the other Warriors did, which meant she had to be ready for anything.

A blast of cold air hit her from behind. She whirled around to see Malcolm, the window open behind him.

"Weather willna stop the enemy," he stated as he stalked toward her.

Her breath hitched in her lungs as she gazed at his windswept golden blond hair. A lock landed against the scar on his face, his azure eyes blazing with hunger. His power exhilarated her. Snow clung to his eyelashes, clothes, and hair and swirled around them in the room. She gazed at his broad shoulders and the way his thin sweater molded to his thickly muscled chest. She knew how tender and loving his arms felt around her.

In two strides, he was before her. There were no words as he yanked her against him, his mouth descending on hers in a kiss that scorched her from the inside out. As her passion grew, the kiss turned more heated, more fervent.

More needy.

He ended the kiss and pressed his forehead to hers. He was as breathless as she when he said, "It's too cold for you."

"I'm on fire."

She barely got the words out before he had her against the wall, their bodies rubbing against each other as they yanked, pulled, and tore their clothes to get them off. Malcolm gathered her against him, sat on the floor, and then lay back so she straddled him.

Evie bit back a gasp when her bare skin met the cold stones. The chill only lasted a moment because Malcolm's hands slowly ran up her legs to her hips then her waist until he cupped her breasts. A sigh fell from her lips when he began thumbing her nipples. The desire shot straight down to her center, making it pulse. She needed him inside her. Now.

She rose to her knees and took his cock in hand, guiding him to her entrance. His eyes darkened when she lowered herself onto his length until she had taken all of him. Only then did she begin moving her hips. Malcolm sat up, holding her firmly against him as he captured her lips in a searing kiss, their bodies moving against each other, creating the friction they both needed.

"Evie," he whispered against her mouth.

She dug her nails into his back as the desire tightened.

Their tempo increased. She tore her lips from his in an effort to drag more air into her lungs. Her head fell back as her climax crept closer and closer each time he moved inside her. His large hand splayed across her back, keeping her close so their bodies slid against each other.

A gasp of surprise fell from her lips when Malcolm's hand fisted in her hair. Then his lips wrapped around a nipple. She screamed as the orgasm swallowed her and swept her away, pleasure rolling through her in cresting waves. Malcolm's arms tightened around her as he whispered her name. Then he stiffened as he climaxed.

It took some time before she came back to herself. They remained locked in each other's embrace. Evie opened her eyes and watched the snow dancing around them in the moonlight. She cooled rapidly, but she was loath to move. Still, she couldn't suppress the shiver that went through her.

"Shite," Malcolm said and swiftly got to his feet. He released her and shut the window.

Evie shook as she tried to put on her torn clothing. Malcolm gathered their garments before lifting her into his arms. She huddled against him, seeking his warmth as he rushed down the stairs. In no time, he had them ensconced in their room. He threw back the duvet and deposited her in the bed as he added more logs to the fire. Then he was under the covers with her, holding her tight.

"How do you stay so warm?" she asked as she pressed herself against him.

He chuckled while rubbing his hands up and down her back. "I'm sorry. I should've closed the window after I came in."

"I didn't remember either." She looked at him with a grin. "I was thinking of other things."

His azure eyes darkened. "Aye," he whispered.

"I know what will warm me up. You."

"Ah, lass. You're my match in every way."

She pulled his head down for a kiss as she sank her fingers into his hair. He rolled atop her as his cock thickened between them. As fire licked through her body once more, there were no other thoughts of cold.

"I love you," she whispered as he slid inside her.

BACON-WRAPPED STUFFED JALAPEÑOS

COOK TIME:

Prep: 15 min
Cook: 20 min
Total: 35 min

SERVINGS:

8 jalapeños

INGREDIENTS:

- 8 large jalapeños, seeds removed
- 8 oz cream cheese, softened
- 1 ½ cups cheese of choice, grated
- ¼ cup green onions, sliced
- 1/8 cup cilantro, chopped
- 8 slices of bacon

<u>**INSTRUCTIONS:**</u>

1. Preheat oven to 350°F
2. Fry bacon until it starts to get crisp. Remove and place on a plate lined with paper towels.
3. Slice just a little off the top, lengthwise, of each jalapeño, spooning out the seeds and hollowing out the pepper. Rinse jalapeños and discard any loose seeds that may remain.
4. Dry jalapeños and place them on a baking sheet.
5. In a medium bowl, beat cream cheese for 2 minutes, then add grated cheese, onions, and cilantro.
6. Spoon cheese mixture into each jalapeño and place back on baking sheet.
7. Wrap bacon around each pepper and secure with a couple of toothpicks.
8. Pop into the oven and bake for 18-20 minutes.
9. Remove and enjoy!

DALE AND RENNIE

Dale stopped the car on the side of the road. The entrance to MacLeod Castle was in a few hundred yards. It was hidden, but Fallon's directions had been quite clear.

"You can change your mind."

He turned his head to the side and looked into Rennie's green eyes. "I know."

"Do you want to go back home?"

His gaze slid back to the road.

Rennie's hand gently rested on his arm. "Honey, the invitation came out of nowhere. You've never heard from them before now."

"What if they doona send another invite?"

"Then they're arseholes who don't deserve to know you."

He smiled as he glanced at her. Leave it to his amazing woman to put it so bluntly. But his smile vanished quickly. "I want this."

"Then why aren't you driving?" She sighed and let her

hand fall away. "You're a different man than the one you were before we met. Obviously, they know that."

"They've been watching me." He couldn't know that for sure, but he'd do it if he were in their shoes.

Rennie shifted in her seat to face him. She had her dark brown waves pulled back in a bun, and long bangs tangled in her lashes. "Maybe. I say they've waited too long to get to know you. Then again, I didn't witness what happened before. I have your stories. And they have theirs. You told me they were good, decent people. It's not like they asked us to come just to kill us."

He briefly squeezed his eyes closed before looking at her. "That's where your imagination went?"

"I read a lot," she said with a shrug as if that explained everything.

And, in a way, it did.

"If they wanted me dead, they would've killed me a long time ago."

Rennie put her hand atop his on the gearshift. "They haven't. Instead, they asked us here. So, drive, honey. Let's get there, because I need out of this car before my bladder bursts."

Dale chuckled and pressed the accelerator. He drove to where the road curved and then turned the wheel slightly to the other side, just as Fallon had instructed. They drove off the road and passed through the shield.

"My goodness," Rennie whispered in awe as she caught sight of the castle through the trees.

Once clear of the forest, they got their first good look at the castle. It had been a long time since he'd seen it, but it was still just as beautiful. Maybe even more so with the snow.

"Wow. Just…wow," Rennie murmured.

Dale's heart thudded in his chest. He couldn't remember the last time he had been this nervous. He parked his vehicle next to others and found his hands shaking as he got out of the car. It was a clear, cold morning. The sunlight reflected off the newly fallen snow, making it sparkle. The sound of gulls and puffins could be heard in the distance, as well as the crashing of waves. He tilted his head back and gazed at the imposing structure of the castle before him.

Rennie's hand slid into his as she came up beside him. He turned his head to her and grinned. Given all the things he had done, he never once allowed himself to believe that he deserved love—especially not from a Druid like her. But she had helped him see that he *did* deserve it. It had been a long process because he'd had a lot of emotional and mental healing to do. She had stayed beside him the entire time, lending him her strength and enveloping him in love.

He might have wanted to tread the path of good, but it was only with her help that he had succeeded.

"As pretty as this is, I'm freezing. And I have to pee," she told him with a twinkle in her eyes.

Before Dale could reply, the opening castle door drew his attention. He froze when he spotted the MacLeod brothers. The trio walked out onto the steps of the castle, shoulder to shoulder. It had been years since he had seen them last, but he would've recognized them anywhere.

"Welcome," Lucan said with a smile. "We're glad to have you both."

Dale felt Rennie tug on his hand as she walked toward the brothers. His feet felt like bricks as he trudged after her. He scanned the area, looking for other Warriors in case this was a trap.

"Hello," Rennie said when they reached the brothers. "I'm Rennie."

"Nice to meet you. I'm Quinn. I should also warn you there are a bunch of us. We willna hold it against you if you doona remember all our names."

Rennie laughed and turned to Fallon. Dale didn't hear what they said. Blood rushed in his ears. His memories took him back to a different time when the MacLeods and everyone associated with them had been his enemies.

Someone firmly grasping his shoulder jerked him out of his thoughts. Dale blinked and looked into Fallon's dark green eyes. Was this when they told him the invitation had all been a ruse? Would they exact their revenge on him now?

"The past is in the past," Fallon said in a low voice. Behind him, Quinn and Lucan kept Rennie occupied. "We have the best of intentions. You and Rennie are safe here and among friends."

Friends. That certainly wasn't a word he'd thought to connect to the Warriors and Druids of MacLeod Castle. Dale swallowed and released a breath. "How did you know?"

"That you were thinking about the past? Or that this might be a trap?" Fallon shrugged and then grinned. "Because I would be doing the same."

"What I did—"

"Doesna need to be discussed," Fallon interrupted him. "No' by us, that is. If you need to talk about it, we willna stop you."

Dale nodded, understanding dawning. "But this is a celebration."

"Exactly." Then the eldest MacLeod moved to the side and said loudly enough so Rennie could hear, "This is an informal event. We're a loud, unruly bunch, so please make yourselves at home. If you want a tour of the castle, we'll be happy to make that happen. Mingle, eat, and drink until it's time for the Yule celebration."

Rennie wasn't oblivious to the private exchange between Dale and Fallon. Dale had looked more relaxed after, so she was grateful for whatever the elder MacLeod had said that'd helped put him at ease.

Her stomach tightened as she followed Quinn inside the castle to a restroom. When she returned, Dale was on her heels as they went farther inside. She knew about the Warriors and Druids, and she had hoped to meet them one day, but she had never expected it to be so soon. Knowing that she was about to face other immortals like Dale and their Druid counterparts, she was more than a little nervous.

Her gaze swept the castle, noting the beautiful rugs, ancient weapons, and tapestries hanging on the walls, interspersed with new artwork. It was a mix of old and new everywhere she looked. It shouldn't have worked, but it did. Beautifully. She could easily explore the castle for days and want to start all over again. There was just so much to see.

Quinn talked, but she only listened with half an ear because she was too busy gazing in wonder at everything.

"You're gawking," Dale whispered in her ear.

She shot him a look and playfully hit him. "I can't help it. This place is amazing."

"Thank you," Lucan said, pleasure on his face at her compliment.

Suddenly, they were in the great hall, the ceiling soaring above them. There was a massive hearth, one so big that she could walk into it without bending. Tables with chairs were set in a U-shape in the middle of the room. And off to the side was the largest Christmas tree she had ever seen. But the decorations didn't end there. Lighted and decorated garland was everywhere.

"We tend to go all out," said a petite woman with long, black hair and the bluest eyes Rennie had ever seen. The Druid held out her hand. "I'm Isla."

Then, introductions took some time. Rennie met each of the Druids and their Warrior husbands. Not once did anyone show any kind of disdain or contempt for her or Dale. The relief was so substantial that she got lightheaded. Dale steadied her by tightening his arm around her. When she looked at him, he gave her a soft smile, telling her that he knew exactly what had happened.

The women welcomed her easily, and Rennie was soon drawn into conversations with them. She listened as they told her story after story. She laughed long and hard at many of them. When she glanced up, she found Dale with the men. She hadn't realized they had moved away from each other. It had happened slowly, but they had been welcomed so warmly that it was easy to relax and enjoy the day.

"We're really glad you both came," Ronnie said.

Cara nodded. "We should've done this sooner."

"I feel bad that we didn't," Reaghan stated.

Rennie shook her head. "Please, don't. I'm a firm believer that things happen when they're supposed to. However, I do want to say that Dale needed this. So, thank you all, from the bottom of my heart."

"Stop. All of you," Aisley said with a glower. "I forgot my waterproof mascara, and if you all keep talking like this, I'm going to cry."

Larena chuckled. "Going to cry? I already am."

"Oh, for Pete's sake," Tara grumbled and wiped at her eyes.

Aisley grunted and dabbed at her face with the sleeve of her shirt.

Rennie looked at the fourteen women around her and realized she could be friends with them. Not acquaintances, but real friends who kept in contact weekly. The kind who met up for lunches, went shopping, and had girls' weekends.

Her head swiveled to look at Dale. He was laughing and seemed at ease, as if he had been friends with them for years. Her heart swelled at the sight. He had needed this—more than he'd realized. Because no matter how many times she told him that he was a different man now, he never truly believed her. There had always been a nugget of doubt in his mind that he would never be able to shake off his past. But here, now, surrounded by those who had once been his enemies, they might actually be able to see the wonderful, kind, loving man that he was—regardless of his past mistakes.

As if sensing her gaze, he turned his head, and his dark

eyes met hers. He mouthed: *I love you*. She grinned and mouthed it back.

This was the start of something new for both of them.

"It's time," Sonya said.

Rennie checked her phone to see that they had been talking for hours. "Time for what?"

"Come," Laura said with a grin. "We'll show you."

Rennie followed the group from the hall into a back room. There was a table with ivy hair wreaths. Each of the women took one and set it atop their heads until only one remained.

Saffron lifted the circlet. "We made this for you. You don't have to wear it."

"I want to," she said hurriedly.

Saffron smiled and gently set it on Rennie's hair. She reached up and touched it. Then the other woman turned her to face a mirror on the wall so she could see her reflection.

"I take that smile to mean you like it," Marcail said.

Rennie blinked the sudden moisture from her eyes. "Very much."

"We'd better get to the food before it's all gone," Gwynn said into the silence that followed.

Dani came up beside Rennie and explained. "We set out food so everyone can grab whatever they wish. There is also mead since that's what we prefer during these celebrations, but there will be other choices, as well, both alcoholic and non-alcoholic. I should warn you about Galen. He has a pit for a stomach. He's never full. Which means we like to get there before he does."

"I've hidden food before," Evie said.

Reaghan snorted loudly. "I hide food from my husband every day."

Everyone burst out laughing as they made their way to the kitchen.

Rennie was shocked at the amount of food spread around the kitchen. There was everything anyone could possibly want. And she tried all of it. Just as the others had warned, Galen was the first of the men into the kitchen. They hadn't been joking about the amount of food he ate.

Dale came up beside her as she stood near a window, eating and watching the others. "I like your hair wreath."

"Me, too," she said with a bright smile. "I'm so glad we came."

"I am, too."

"I've never been to a solstice celebration. I'm eager to see what it's all about."

He smoothed the backs of his knuckles down her cheek. "You willna have long to wait."

"Do you think we'll be invited back?"

Dale nodded his head of thick, dark hair. "We already have been."

She gazed into his dark eyes. "Are you happy?"

"More than you could imagine."

Rennie leaned against him and shared her plate of food. Yes, this was a new beginning for them.

CANDY CANE MARTINI

INGREDIENTS:

- 1 oz vanilla vodka
- 1 oz crème de cacao
- 1 oz peppermint schnapps
- ¼ oz grenadine
- 1 oz half and half
- 1 candy cane, crushed for garnish

INSTRUCTIONS:

1. Fill a cocktail shaker with ice and add vanilla
   vodka, crème de cacao, and peppermint schnapps.
   Shake until very cold. About 20-30 seconds.
2. Add half and half. Swirl to combine.
3. In a chilled martini glass, pour grenadine into the
   bottom and swirl around the edges.

4. Strain and pour candy cane martini into the glass. Add crushed candy cane to garnish.

5. Sip and enjoy responsibly.

<u>NOTES:</u>

- Always use high-quality ice to make any cocktail.
- If you don't have vanilla vodka, plain, whipped cream, or peppermint vodka will work.
- If you use peppermint vodka, cut back on the peppermint schnapps.
- Crème de menthe will work in place of peppermint schnapps, but it will be green -eliminate the grenadine to keep the color pretty.

The night was cold and clear, and the quarter-moon hung in the inky sky with billions of stars as observers. Between the castle and the cliffs, a massive fire roared, sending sparks dancing into the night.

The longest night of the year was a special celebration. One that Fallon loved to watch. The Druids with their ivy hair wreaths stood in a circle around the fire, their hands joined. Cara had given out mistletoe to everyone as a blessing since the winter fruit of mistletoe was a symbol of life to the Celts in the dark winter months. Fallon and his brothers might not be Druids, but they were well acquainted with the Yule ceremony from their youth.

"Seeing this never gets old," Larena whispered as she joined him.

He wrapped an arm around her and accepted the cup of mead she'd brought for him. Everyone at the castle took part in brewing their own mead. There were different flavors for everyone, which was another reason their family worked. What had Rennie called them? *A found family*.

Aye. He liked that. Because they had found each other and decided to stay together. That made them strong.

"Here it comes," Larena said excitedly. "This is my favorite part."

Fallon listened as the Druids began their chant of gratitude and thanks for the year and for the one that was to come. As their voices grew, the flames of the fire licked higher and higher as if trying to reach the stars.

The Druids' magic washed over each of them before expanding and covering everything that made up MacLeod land. Of all the seasonal Druid celebrations, the winter solstice was his favorite. Was it the weather? The deep, dark of the night? Perhaps it was something else entirely. He didn't know or care.

He looked at Larena, who had her hair wreath atop her head of golden blond hair. She met his gaze as a slow smile curved her lips.

When the Druids ended their chant, Fallon lifted his cup into the air. "To family!"

"To family!" everyone shouted in response.

He took a drink of mead and smiled at his wife beside him, sighing in utter and complete contentment.

CRAB AND GOUDA-STUFFED MUSHROOMS

<u>COOK TIME:</u>

Prep: 30 min
Cook: 30 min
Total: 1 hour

<u>SERVINGS:</u>

18 – 20 mushrooms

<u>INGREDIENTS:</u>

- 24 oz cremini mushrooms, about 2 inches in diameter, cleaned
- ¼ cup olive oil, divided
- 1/3 cup sliced scallions, plus additional for garnish
- 2 garlic cloves, minced
- 4 oz cream cheese

- 2 teaspoons Worcestershire sauce
- 1 teaspoon Dijon mustard
- 1 teaspoon Old Bay seasoning
- 2 tablespoons grated parmesan
- 1 cup shredded Gouda, divided
- 6 oz lump crab meat
- Salt and pepper to taste
- Lemon wedges for serving
- Optional – hot sauce, to taste

INSTRUCTIONS:

1. Preheat oven to 400°F with rack in the middle position.
2. Remove stems from mushrooms and set aside. Use a small spoon to gently hollow out a small portion of the mushroom cavities, removing gills.
3. On a lined baking sheet, toss mushroom caps with 2 tablespoons olive oil and a few pinches of salt and pepper. Arrange mushrooms in a single layer, cavity-side down. Roast for about 15 minutes until liquid is released. Remove from oven, drain liquid from pan, and flip caps. Set aside.
4. While mushrooms are roasting, finely chop stems. Heat remaining 2 tablespoons of oil in a nonstick skillet until simmering.
5. Add chopped stems with ¼ teaspoon each of salt and pepper, and cook, stirring often, until liquid is released, and mushrooms are soft but not brown— about 5 minutes.

6. In a bowl, mix cream cheese, Dijon mustard, and Worcestershire sauce. Stir in mushroom mixture, parmesan cheese, ½ cup shredded Gouda, and seafood seasoning. Gently stir in crab meat, breaking up any large pieces. Season to taste with salt and pepper and hot sauce (if using).

7. Fill roasted mushroom caps with filling mixture, packing it into the cavity and mounding slightly. Top each mushroom with remaining Gouda.

8. Bake for 5 – 7 minutes until cheese is melted and filling is heated through. Serve hot, topped with additional sliced scallions and a squeeze of lemon juice.

THANK YOU

Thank you for reading **HOLIDAY HEAT.** I hope you loved these stories as much as I loved writing them. Next is a special prequel in the Dragon Kings/Dark Kings series, IGNITE THE MAGIC.

Passion's magic ignites a fire too hot to touch—and too wicked to die…

If you love the Dragon Kings series, you'll love the upcoming Dark Universe book set in the Skye Druids series, HEART OF GLASS…

A desire that won't be denied.

To find out when new books release
SIGN UP FOR MY NEWSLETTER today at
http://www.tinyurl.com/DonnaGrantNews

Join my Facebook group, Donna Grant Groupies, for
exclusive giveaways and sneak peeks of future books.
http://bit.ly/DGGroupies

Keep reading for a glimpse at IGNITE THE MAGIC and a
peek at HEART OF GLASS…

NEXT IN THE DRAGON KINGS/DARK KINGS WORLD

IGNITE THE MAGIC, DRAGON KINGS STANDALONE PREQUEL

New York Times and *USA Today* bestselling author Donna Grant delivers an epic prequel to her long-running and critically acclaimed Dark Universe series.

Passion's magic ignites a fire too hot to touch—and too wicked to die…

The stars have always called to Ailis, beckoning her to see what other realms were out there. She's told its impossible, but that doesn't stop her need to explore beyond what others believe. Ailis never expected to change history by creating the first doorway to another realm. She certainly never imagined opening that door to find a commanding dragon who shifts into a man. She's irresistibly drawn to Lennox, powerless against the yearning of her body and the longing of her heart.

Magic might have chosen Lennox as King of Dragon Kings, but it's a position he's never wanted. Until the day a new being arrives—and irrevocably changes his life. The closer he gets to the fearless, ravishing woman, the more he fights the passion that flares between them. He lives only for his duty, but one fiery kiss unleashes a firestorm of desire that will ripple across eons and realms. Fate might have brought them together, but will it also tear them apart?

The origins of the Dark Kings/Dragon Kings and the entire Dark Universe is finally revealed.

New York Times and *USA Today* bestselling author Donna Grant returns to the beautiful and mysterious Isle of Skye with a captivating tale of magic, mystery, and unexpected passion.

A desire that won't be denied.

Ferne Crawford is a Seer with unique abilities that set her apart from other Druids. She once ignored her magic with tragic results. So, when she's bombarded with visions of a great evil that call her to a place she's been warned never to go, she's powerless to resist. Her life takes a drastic turn the moment she arrives on Skye and encounters a handsome, valiant stranger. Theo makes her ache for his touch. Their meeting stirs an explosive passion, awakening a yearning that only he can satisfy. However, there's more than the malice which brought her to the isle that intends her harm.

Detective Inspector Theo Frasier carries the weight of the isle and his people on his shoulders. With more Druid murders and no leads on who's controlling the killing mist, he's beginning to feel the strain. The last thing he needs is anything—or anyone—distracting him. But once he meets Ferne, he can't get her out of his head. Or his heart. She fills his every thought, day and night. His need for her consumes him, pushing everything else aside. But will his love be enough to save them from the growing threat?

ABOUT THE AUTHOR

New York Times and *USA Today* bestselling author Donna Grant has been praised for her "totally addictive" and "unique and sensual" stories. She's written more than one hundred novels spanning multiple genres of romance including the bestselling Dark King series that features a thrilling combination of Dragon Kings, Druids, Fae, and immortal Highlanders who are dark, dangerous, and irresistible. She lives in Texas with her dog and a cat.

www.DonnaGrant.com
www.MotherofDragonsBooks.com

facebook.com/AuthorDonnaGrant

instagram.com/dgauthor

bookbub.com/authors/donna-grant

amazon.com/Donna-Grant/e/B00279DJGE

pinterest.com/donnagrant1

www.ingramcontent.com/pod-product-compliance
Lightning Source LLC
Chambersburg PA
CBHW011220190726
48287CB00008B/2691

9 781958 353202